Everafter

ALSO BY
ELIZABETH CHANDLER

Kissed by an Angel
KISSED BY AN ANGEL, THE POWER OF LOVE, and SOULMATES

Evercrossed
a KISSED BY AN ANGEL novel

Everlasting
a KISSED BY AN ANGEL novel

Dark Secrets 1
LEGACY OF LIES and DON'T TELL

Dark Secrets 2
NO TIME TO DIE and THE DEEP END OF FEAR

The Back Door of Midnight
a DARK SECRETS novel

Everafter

A Kissed by an Angel novel

Elizabeth Chandler

Simon Pulse

New York   London   Toronto   Sydney   New Delhi

alloy**entertainment**
Produced by Alloy Entertainment
151 West 26th Street, New York, NY 10001

SIMON PULSE
An imprint of Simon & Schuster Children's Publishing Division
1230 Avenue of the Americas, New York, NY 10020
First Simon Pulse hardcover edition March 2013

For information about special discounts for bulk purchases, please
contact Simon & Schuster Special Sales at 1-866-506-1949 or
business@simonandschuster.com.

The Simon & Schuster Speakers Bureau can bring authors to your live event.
For more information or to book an event contact the
Simon & Schuster Speakers Bureau at 1-866-248-3049 or visit our website at
www.simonspeakers.com.

The text of this book was set in Versailles.

Manufactured in the United States of America

2 4 6 8 10 9 7 5 3 1

CIP Data is available from the Library of Congress.

ISBN 978-1-4424-0918-7
ISBN 978-1-4424-0922-4 (eBook)

To my husband, Bob,
now and everafter

Prologue

EVEN GREGORY WAS STUNNED BY THE DEADLY explosion of his hate. If only he had struck *Ivy*—that was Gregory's first thought.

Emerging from an exhausted darkness, he recalled with pleasure the scene at the beach: a cocky lifeguard scanning the sea for someone to save, suddenly struck down by lightning—*his* lightning. Forced to leave Beth suddenly, Gregory had seethed with anger, and his demonic fury had been glorious, an electric show of deadly might.

Still, the lightning event had ended too quickly.

Hovering over the lifeguard, staring down at the pattern of a metal chain and cross burned into his victim's chest, Gregory had realized that death itself was rather dull. The dying was the interesting part. The scent of fear in the victim and the horror in those who looked on, these were the kinds of things that could ease his hellish pain.

Despite his power, Gregory longed to have back his human abilities. He needed a reliable servant, someone whose mind wouldn't fight him the way Beth's had. Happily, Ivy mixed with all kinds of people, even a guy the police were chasing for murder.

A tantalizing thought took hold of Gregory's spirit: What if, using Ivy's new friend, he could deceive her, drive her to despair, and drag her down to hell?

Now. Ever. Ours. The voices were speaking to him again.

What if he could destroy her hope of ever joining Tristan in heaven?

The power is within you.

The voices were wise, Gregory thought; they knew him better than he knew himself.

Vengeance is mine!

One

WAS HE STILL ALIVE? IVY WONDERED AS SHE STARED down at the wilting bouquets of funeral flowers. If Tristan had died, would her heart know it?

"Ivy, are you okay?" Dhanya called to her, then opened the gate between the old Harwich church and its cemetery.

Earlier, they had attended the funeral for Michael Steadman and served at the reception that followed. It had been hard for Ivy to look at the faces of the lifeguard's family and friends, most of them still in shock. The minister had preached on a biblical quote about seeing through a glass darkly, telling them to trust in God's inscrutable will. But Ivy feared that the deadly lightning bolt had been an act of Gregory, not God.

Six weeks ago, not long after Ivy, Dhanya, Beth, and Beth's cousin Kelsey had arrived at the Seabright Inn, the girls had held a séance. They were just fooling around, but looking back now, Ivy knew that was when Gregory's spirit had reentered the world. Beth, who was psychic and the gentlest, most open person Ivy had ever known, had been the most vulnerable; Gregory had possessed her, forcing her to attack Ivy. It had taken the combined strength of Ivy, Beth, and Will to expel Gregory.

Beth had gone home to Connecticut to recover. In the last four days, Will and Ivy had seen no sign of Gregory on the Cape, but the demon knew how to hide himself. Ivy's great fear in searching for Tristan was that she would not only reveal to Gregory that Tristan had returned, she would lead the police—and worse, the treacherous Bryan—to "Luke McKenna," the body which Tristan now occupied.

Yesterday, the Cape Cod police had contacted Ivy, hot on the trail of their suspected murderer. From that, Ivy drew hope that Tristan was still alive. The authorities hadn't found his—"Luke's"—body.

Dhanya joined Ivy at the grave of Gregory's latest victim. "Aunt Cindy said the Steadmans are leaving the Cape." The Seabright's owner, Beth and Kelsey's aunt, was close friends with Mrs. Steadman. "How will they ever go to the beach again?" Dhanya said sadly. "How will they ever enjoy summer again?"

She and Ivy began to walk. The mid-July sun warmed the silent churchyard, reflecting off the newest and shiniest gravestones. Here and there, a tall tree allowed dappled light to fall on the older memorials, stones splattered with lichen and leaning at odd angles. Ivy paused to run her finger across the top of one of these, marveling that such gentle, slow-growing things as tree roots had the strength to topple granite.

"Cemeteries are lovely places," Dhanya remarked, watching two butterflies alight on purple phlox, "as long as you don't know anyone buried there."

That made Ivy laugh out loud.

"Dhanya! Ivy! Over here," Kelsey called to them.

They turned, surprised. Their roommate, who was supposed to be working at the inn with Will, was stretched out on a sunny spot near the center of the cemetery. "I've got big news. You're not going to believe it!"

"What I can't believe is that you're taking a sunbath on somebody's grave," Dhanya replied.

Kelsey laughed and rested her back against the stone, her athletic legs extended straight out in front of her and glistened with tanning oil. She combed her fingers through a mass of wavy auburn hair, then gestured to the markers on either side. "Have a seat. Rest in peace. You guys have earned it."

Instead, Dhanya chose a stone bench and sat down gracefully. She had a dancer's body and a long dark curtain of hair. If she had rested her chin on her hand, Ivy thought, she would have resembled a classic monument to grief.

Ivy sat on a marble curb that marked the border of a family plot.

"Did you hear from Bryan?" Ivy asked.

"He came over before heading to the ice rink."

Dhanya looked disgusted. "Kelsey, you swore you wouldn't even glance at Bryan after he stood you up and ignored your texts all weekend."

"But it turned out he had a good reason," Kelsey answered, her voice rising with excitement. "Saturday night, he jumped off the train bridge—the one over the Cape Cod Canal."

"What?!" Ivy exclaimed, sounding shocked, though she had witnessed the incident.

"That's his excuse?" Dhanya said, unimpressed.

"Dhanya, the bridge was going up," Kelsey explained. "He leaped fifty feet down to the canal. Think about it—he could have broken his back and drowned if he'd landed the wrong way in the water."

It was what Ivy feared for Tristan. Standing on the canal bank, she had lost sight of him.

"You'll never guess why Bryan was up there," Kelsey went on. "He was chasing Luke."

"Luke!" Dhanya moved over to sit on the marble curb with Ivy. "Did you know he was still on the Cape?"

"I haven't seen or heard from Luke since June," Ivy lied.

"So Luke's now in jail?" Dhanya asked Kelsey.

"No. Missing in action. Bryan's been looking for him."

And if he finds him, he'll kill him, Ivy thought. What kind of story had Bryan concocted for the police and Kelsey?

"Why did Bryan chase Luke?" Ivy asked aloud. "I thought they were good friends."

"Not anymore," Kelsey replied. "Bryan believes that Luke murdered that girl, the one police said jumped from the bridge a week ago—Alice something or other."

Alicia Crowley, Ivy thought. Bryan had already framed Luke for Corinne's death. Now he was adding Alicia to the list.

"She was close to Luke," Kelsey added. "Luke sure likes to knock off his girlfriends."

Dhanya shivered. "That could have been *you,* Ivy."

Ivy simply shook her head. Her roommates condemned and feared the wrong person. But Bryan had already proven his willingness to kill anyone who learned the dark truth about him. To warn Kelsey and Dhanya—and Beth and Will—would only put them in greater danger.

The way to keep everyone safe from Bryan was for

her to find the evidence that would place him behind bars, the evidence that would clear Luke's name. Then she and Tristan could be together, and Tristan could find a way to redeem himself. If he was still alive.

Tristan, where are you? Ivy cried silently, though she knew, alive or not, her fallen angel could no longer hear her heart calling to him.

TRISTAN AWOKE IN DARKNESS. FOR A MOMENT HE had no idea where he was. His clothes were wet; the tarp he was lying on was damp and gritty. The place reeked.

Unable to see a thing, he sat up and stretched out his hands. To his right and left, his fingers brushed against something moist and hard, surfaces that felt like rough plastic, walls that slanted away from him. He realized then that he was rocking slightly, and heard a quiet *lap-lap*. He was entombed in the hull of a boat, at anchor on calm water. He suddenly remembered the old lobster boat he had swum to, recognizing at least three ingredients of the stench: rotted fish, machine oil, and mildew.

He had walked more than forty miles the last two nights, working his way from the Cape Cod Canal to Nauset Harbor, close to where Ivy was staying. There were no private docks or marinas here; the boats were moored in a bay protected from the Atlantic's fury by a long finger of dunes and small islands at the northern end of Nauset Beach.

Everafter

Before sunrise Tuesday morning, Tristan had spotted this dilapidated boat among the commercial fishing craft and pleasure boats anchored here. Hidden among the trees, he had watched it all day, as the other boats departed then returned through Nauset Inlet, but no one had claimed it.

After nightfall, overwhelmed by a need to sleep undisturbed, he had swum out to the boat. Its curved, low-slung sides made it easy to board. The lobster traps piled in the stern were tagged with plastic rings that bore expiration dates from the previous December. Checking the vessel from stern to bow, Tristan had figured it was more likely that the boat would sink than its owner suddenly show up.

He'd retreated to the wheelhouse, a three-sided shelter with large square windows. When a party had begun on a boat a hundred yards off, he descended to the snug but smelly quarters below. He figured he had slept for several hours and was glad to emerge now into the fresh air of the open deck.

Looking south, he could barely discern the rise of dark land against the starlit sky, the bluffs on which the Seabright perched. He longed to be with Ivy, but he couldn't chance it, not yet. It had been three weeks since his picture had made page one of the *Cape Cod Times*, but the stare of a Walmart security guard had been enough to deter him from buying a new cell phone. His old one and the watch Ivy had given him lay at the bottom of the canal. All he had in his pockets now was a soggy bankroll—from Bryan when he was pretending to be Luke's friend—and a gold coin with an angel stamped on each side, a gift from Philip.

"Catch anything?"

Tristan swung around, startled. Lacey sat on an upside-down work bucket, fully materialized.

"A lobster? A murderer?" she asked.

"An angel," he replied, though her angelic purple shimmer was apparent only in the tint of her long dark hair. Dressed in a tank top and ripped leggings, she didn't look like a local, but at least she wasn't wearing one of her theatrical getups. Both as an angel and a B-movie teen star, Lacey had always enjoyed grabbing the attention of an audience.

"You weren't fishing for me," she said. "I haven't heard a syllable from you, and you know that I can't locate people unless they call to me."

"You found me anyway," he pointed out.

"I narrowed it down to two places, hell or here. You landed here, flying like a moth to Ivy's flame."

"Have you seen her?" he asked quickly, hoping Lacey had been sticking close to Ivy despite the scorn she usually heaped on their relationship. "How is she?"

"For you, as dangerous as ever."

"No," Tristan said firmly. This was why he hadn't called out to Lacey.

"Tristan, I was there on the bridge with you and Bryan.

I heard the voices. They were as loud as the night Gregory fell to his death. Time may be running out. You need to redeem yourself."

Tristan gazed at the stars, as if he could read the time off the bright face of heaven's clock. "Could you tell what the voices were saying?" he asked. For him, they always began the same way, a low murmuring, overlapping waves of menacing voices, their emotions clearer than their words.

"Their words were meant for you."

"Meaning you couldn't decipher them," he guessed.

"And you can?"

He nodded. The words were becoming increasingly clear to him.

"That's not a good sign! First you're stripped of your angelic powers; now you're hearing the words of demons!" But Lacey's curiosity got the better of her. "What did they say?"

"*Now. Ever. Ours.* And when I was up on the bridge, *Which way?* They kept asking me, *Which way?*"

"Their way," Lacey said. "Gregory's way."

"I have to stop him. He'll kill Ivy."

Lacey grabbed Tristan by the shoulders. As solid as the angel looked and felt, her grip lacked strength, and he easily pulled away from her.

"Listen to me, Tristan. It's you who needs protecting. Go to the police. Turn yourself in as Luke. Let them arrest you and keep you locked up safe. If Bryan kills you before you've redeemed yourself, you're damned. You'll be in hell forever."

"The way to redeem myself is to expel Gregory from this world. I can't do that from prison."

"How are you going to get rid of a demon," she replied sarcastically, "ask him nicely to go home?"

"If Gregory possesses a person's mind and that person dies, Gregory is banished forever. You told me that yourself."

"So you're going to knock somebody off?" She moved her face close to his. "Tristan, you *can't* kill! You can't take away life, and you can't give it back—that's how you got yourself into this mess. Life, its entrances and exits, is scripted by Number One Director, and he doesn't take kindly to us lowly actors messing with his stage directions."

"There's a way to send Gregory back to hell and keep Ivy safe. There must be. That's how I'm supposed to redeem myself."

"No, that's how you *want* to."

"I need you to carry a message to Ivy," he said.

"I won't."

Tristan hurried on. "Warn her about Bryan. He boasted of murdering both Alicia and Corinne, as well as leaving that woman to die in the hit-and-run."

Lacey folded her arms. "The chick's not dumb. I'm sure she's figured that out."

"Okay then, just tell her where I am."

"No! Your love for Ivy is too great a temptation for you. You've proven you can't handle it. If I'm going to help you—"

"Lacey, I don't need or want you to save me."

The angel turned away.

Tristan sighed and reached for her arm. "I'm sorry. It's just that—"

"You've been warned," she said, then faded to a purple haze, blending with the sea mist, and disappeared.

Tristan was on his own. He had to figure out how to reach Ivy. Harder yet, he had to destroy Gregory. That was the only way to keep her safe.

His eyes moved along the shore. In another hour, it would be washed in morning light. "Which way, which way?" he murmured to himself.

Two

WEDNESDAY EVENING, IVY SAT IN HER CAR IN THE inn's parking lot and prayed. "Lacey," she said softly, "where are you? Why haven't you answered my call?"

A thump against the passenger side of her VW made her turn hopefully.

"Too bad about your car," Bryan said.

Ivy climbed out slowly and deliberately, determined not to show fear.

He strolled around to the driver's side. "You've got some damage on the side and rear."

Ignoring him, she shifted the car seat forward, attempting to retrieve her bag of music from the back. He blocked her, using his powerful physique to intimidate.

"Excuse me," she said firmly.

Lounging against the car, Bryan ran his finger over one of the deep scratches he had made in its paint when chasing Ivy and Tristan to the train bridge. "Your rental company isn't going to like this."

"It'll be fixed before they see it."

He smiled. "Good girl! You operate the way I do."

"Not often," Ivy replied, slinging her bag over her shoulder and moving toward the path that led to the inn and cottage.

He caught up with her. "If you need someone who'd *die* before he'd tell a client's secret"—Bryan paused, letting his choice of words sink in—"I can recommend a body shop in River Gardens."

Tony's, Ivy thought, where Bryan said he had gotten his car repaired after the hit-and-run.

"It's no big deal," she said, pushing ahead on the path.

He caught her by the arm and pulled her back. "I knew I could count on you."

"For *what?*"

"For seeing that some things aren't worth getting excited about."

She lowered her voice in an effort to keep it steady.

"I believe our lists of things that are *worth it* are very different."

He laughed and let her go. "I bet your list includes people—like friends and roommates."

Anyone watching them, anyone who didn't know what she knew about Bryan, would see only the smiling green eyes and playful manners of a guy who liked nothing better than to have a good time.

"You know what I'm capable of, Ivy." His genial face made his words all the more chilling. "Don't make me hurt you."

She wanted to run down the path to the cottage, but she forced herself to walk at an easy pace. "I haven't said a word to anyone," she assured him. "But I'm surprised by what you divulged to the police and Kelsey, telling them you were chasing Luke. I can't believe you called into question Alicia's death, which they were ready to dismiss as suicide. You're inviting attention that we could all do without."

"I had to offer them some excuse after they fished me out of the canal. Those damn helicopters. Too bad they didn't reel in Luke. He jumped before I did."

"Did he?" Ivy replied quickly. "Did he swim away?"

"Don't play dumb, Ivy!"

So maybe Tristan was safe!

"Where is he?" Bryan demanded.

"Several days west of here, I hope."

They stopped at the end of the path near the large garden that separated the inn from the girls' cottage.

"No way," Bryan replied. "Luke's a stupid homing pigeon, always returning to his nest. He'll come back to you."

"But it's too dangerous for him. Just like it is for you and me," Ivy added, wanting to make a point. "The police are watching us both very carefully, Bryan." Right now, it was the only argument she knew that might keep Bryan from killing "Luke" the moment he found him.

"For a while maybe," he said. "But the police have a short attention span, and you and Luke have no evidence against me. The cufflink's at the bottom of the canal, the deepest part of it."

Ivy's heart fell. Their one piece of evidence, gone.

Bryan leaned close to her, reaching for a lock of her hair, twining it around his finger. "If you want to survive this, if you want Luke to, don't tell the cops anything. You may think they can protect you. They may tell you they can, but they're slow and clumsy—and I'm not."

The cottage door opened. Ivy was glad it was Kelsey who'd spotted them; her roommate's jealousy would quickly put an end to this conversation.

Bryan let go of Ivy's hair, then glanced down at her bare arm. "Goose bumps, on a hot day like this!"

Kelsey strode toward them, and Ivy headed for the inn.

Inside the large, square kitchen where the girls and Will began each workday, Beth and Kelsey's aunt was brewing tea.

"Want some? Apple-cranberry," she said, brushing back strands of thick red hair that had fallen out of her French braid. "Though I think I could use something stronger than tea." Her usual crisp button-down shirt was wrinkled. Despite her smile, sun-pinked cheeks, and sprinkle of freckles, she looked exhausted. Food in plastic containers and a key with a large *S* attached to the ring lay on the kitchen table.

"How are the Steadmans?" Ivy asked, guessing it was their key.

"Struggling," Aunt Cindy replied. "They closed up their beach house today and are returning to Boston."

Ivy accepted a cup of tea. "I felt so bad for them. When I saw his little brother and sister at the funeral . . ."

Aunt Cindy nodded. "I appreciate the way you girls and Will have pitched in around here the last several days, especially without Beth."

"No problem."

"As soon as Beth gets back," Aunt Cindy continued, "I want to give Will, Dhanya, and Kelsey some extra days off. How are you holding up?"

"Great," Ivy replied, despite her own sleepless nights.

"I had my extra days off. And we've got the routine down now, which makes it much easier."

Aunt Cindy nodded, then carried the Steadmans' key over to the pegboard of room duplicates. "Almost forgot to tell you," she said, glancing at the staff mailboxes, "I took a phone message for you."

"My mother?" Only their parents were allowed to call on the inn's landline.

Aunt Cindy smiled and returned to the table. "No, a gentleman caller."

"Oh, sorry," Ivy said quickly.

"That's okay. He had such a nice voice, I wished he were calling me. Billy . . . Billy Bigelow."

Ivy caught her breath. When she and Tristan were getting to know each other, he had told her that he, too, enjoyed "classical music"—only his idea of classical music wasn't Mozart or Mahler, but Broadway shows from his parents' collection of musicals. *Carousel* was a favorite, and Billy Bigelow was the romantic lead in the story. Tristan had given himself an alias he knew she'd recognize!

Ivy quickly crossed the kitchen to the wooden cubbyholes and picked up the message slip.

Time: 6:10 p.m.
To: Ivy
From: Billy Bigelow

(203) 555-0138

Vacationing here a few days, borrowing a boat on Nauset Harbor.

Come by when you're free.

"I take it from the glow on your face that this is an invitation you've been hoping for," Aunt Cindy said. "A sweetheart from home?"

Ivy tucked the note in her pocket, smiling. "You might say that!"

TRISTAN SAT ON THE FLOOR OF THE WHEELHOUSE, watching the eastern sky darken, listening and waiting. With his leap into the canal, he had lost Ivy's number, but the Orleans information booth had listed the Seabright Inn, and he'd talked a kid into lending his phone. The last four digits of the number he'd left for Ivy matched the last four of the boat's registration, painted on the bow.

Lying back, hands behind his head, lulled by the water's rhythmic lapping, Tristan fell asleep. He awoke to the whistled melody of a song from *Carousel*. Scrambling to his feet, he whistled back and heard a light bump against the side of the fishing boat. He climbed over a jumble of crusted wire traps. Ivy smiled up at him from the kayak, her hair a gold tangle sparkling with sea mist. *Half mermaid, half angel,* he thought. For a moment they just gazed at each other.

"Billy Bigelow?" she asked.

He laughed, and felt the laughter in every part of his body, the way he always did with her. "I knew you'd find me."

"Permission to board, sir?"

He tossed her a rope and she handed him an oar, then a backpack. When he reached for her, she sprang easily onto the deck. Pulling her close, he buried his face in her damp hair, then kissed the high line of her cheekbone. His mouth found hers in a sweet kiss. "I missed you," he said, losing the last of those words in another, deeper kiss.

He felt her shiver and wrapped his arms around her tightly, as if he could keep all that was evil away from her, as if he could hold them together forever.

"I love you, Ivy."

"I love you, Tristan." They kissed again. "I was so afraid," she said. "You could have drowned!"

"*Drowned*—with you as my swim coach?" he teased.

She laughed and rested her head against his chest.

"I was closer to shore than Bryan," Tristan said, "and I had swum farther downstream from the bridge. Once the police were busy with pulling him out, it was easy for me to slip ashore."

"He said the cufflink is gone. He knew we had it."

"I think he'd trailed us to Gran's. On the bridge, he demanded it." Tristan took a deep breath and let it out slowly. "When he caught up with me, I threw it over his head, so he'd chase it. . . . I'm sorry."

"Sorry? No! It was smart," Ivy insisted. "He would have killed you on the spot. We'll find some other piece of evidence."

Tristan shook his head; the truth was the truth. "We've already searched Corinne's room at home from top to bottom. And her apartment was ransacked."

"So the evidence is somewhere else now."

"At the bottom of the ocean," he replied. "Maybe you've noticed: Bryan likes to leave people and other disposable things in deep water."

"We can't give up, Tristan. If we want to be together, we have to clear Luke's name."

He held her close again and rested his chin on her head. "We have to do a lot more than that."

"When you were on the bridge, did you learn anything new from Bryan?"

Tristan told her what Bryan had admitted—boasted of, actually. A year and a half earlier, when he struck the woman on the side of the road, he left her there to die, prizing his hockey career above her life. He knew he could rely on his old friend Tony to fix his car and not report the drunken hit-and-run, but he hadn't counted on Corinne being at the body shop that morning, working on a photo essay. She'd always been a snoop and a blackmailer, and she found in Bryan's damaged car the custom-made cuff-link he had worn to the sports banquet. Unfortunately for Bryan, the police found the other cufflink at the site of the accident.

As Ivy and Tristan had suspected, Bryan grew tired of paying off Corinne; so he strangled her, framing her old boyfriend, Luke. But Bryan soon realized he couldn't rely on Luke to stay out of police view. He killed him, too, dumping him in the ocean off Chatham. After Ivy and Tristan discovered that Alicia could provide Luke with an alibi, Bryan added her to his list of victims.

"There's evidence somewhere," Ivy said. "The more you kill, the more witnesses and evidence you leave behind. Somebody saw something each time Bryan murdered. Somebody has or knows something very useful to us, but just doesn't realize it."

"Ivy, most of the murders happened months ago, and the more time passes, the harder it is—"

"Stop and think about it," she interrupted. "A lot of people were at Max's party the night Bryan slipped off to kill Luke. A lot of people went to the sports banquet the night of the hit-and-run. . . . Of course! They would have taken photos at the banquet. I bet they hired a photographer to sell pictures to all the proud parents." She laughed and picked up a plastic buoy, shook Tristan's hand, and awarded him the float as if it was a trophy. "Smile," she said. "Your cufflink is showing!"

He laughed with her but quickly grew serious again. Bryan was a threat, Tristan thought, but Gregory was an enemy that no gun or human authority could stop. And Gregory had one goal: to kill Ivy. Who would he possess next? Both Dhanya and Kelsey would give him easy access to Ivy.

"We need to find you a safe place, Tristan, somewhere far from here."

"As long as you're with me," he said.

"No, we need to stay separate—just for a while."

"No way!"

"Bryan's lying low right now, pretending we have a deal," she went on. "But he killed everyone else who knew something that would incriminate him. Why would he spare us?"

"Because," Tristan said, "from the police's point of view, Bryan is friends with too many corpses."

"Tristan, don't you see? That's exactly how he'll use us—to cover himself and neatly tie together the murders of Corinne and Alicia. He can finally get his frame-up of Luke to work if he kills us together, so neither of us can talk. He'll make it look like a murder-suicide, the end of Luke's killing spree against the women he loved. The way to stop Bryan is to put distance between you and me—"

"I'll never leave you!"

"Tristan," she pleaded. "We want the same thing, to be together. But for a while we need to be apart."

"I've been apart from you. I won't leave you again."

Ivy closed her eyes and leaned against him, silent for several minutes. At last she said, "Does this boat sail? If I brought fuel for it, could it go?"

Tristan shook his head. "I don't know anything about boat engines, but the electronics are stripped."

"Then you'll be safer on land. Here your only escape is to swim."

"I could go back to Nickerson."

"No, too many park rangers have seen your photo." She hesitated, then said, "I know a place close by that you could use. The family has just left there and Aunt Cindy has the key. It's hanging on the pegboard—I can make a copy."

"How long will they be gone?"

"I don't know. Their son was killed on the beach the afternoon Gregory left Beth. He was struck by a bolt of lightning."

Tristan took a step back from Ivy and stared at her, horrified. "Gregory will kill anyone!" But he knew there was one person in particular he wanted to kill.

Fear and anger ground a fist in Tristan's gut. Unlike Bryan, Gregory wouldn't be cowed by the threat of getting caught. Ivy's safety depended on him. He would destroy Gregory if it was the last thing he did.

Three

"BETH'S BACK!"

Late Thursday morning, Ivy looked up from the bed she was making and grinned. Will, who had the day off, stood outside the window of the barn suite, his tan body glistening with seawater, his hair spiky. "When you're done, meet us on the beach steps," he said.

Twenty minutes later, Ivy crossed the lawn that lay between the inn and the edge of the sandy, shrub-covered bluffs. Beth and Will stood on the landing that was halfway down the steps, looking out at the glittering ocean. From her view at the top, Ivy's eyes traveled to her left, where the sea swept around a long point of land, pooling behind the line of dunes to make Nauset Harbor. She said a prayer for Tristan. She had told him she wouldn't be back until she had copied the key to the beach house, not wanting to draw more attention to the fishing boat until he was ready to leave it.

Beth turned suddenly, as if the psychic part of her had sensed Ivy approaching. Ivy rushed down the steps.

"Whoa! Slow down!" Will exclaimed. "I can't catch both of you."

Ivy hugged Beth. "I'm so glad to see you."

"Me too! I mean, I'm glad to see *you*," Beth said, and they laughed.

Beth's blue eyes were without the shadow that had darkened them when Gregory possessed her. Her light brown hair, streaked with summer sun, lay softly against her apple cheeks. "How are you feeling?" Ivy asked.

"Good, really good. How about you?"

"Great, now that you're back. We missed you!"

Ivy sat on a bench and Beth joined her. Will sat across from them, his paddle and board propped against the railing.

"I missed you, too, but I had you with me," Beth said, lightly touching the pendant that Ivy and Will had given her.

Ivy squeezed Beth's hand, then looked across at Will.

She remembered the fear and pain that had lined his face when they found Beth in the bell tower with a rope around her neck. She remembered the agony in his voice: *Ivy, if I lose her, I can't go on!* Now his brown eyes were shining.

Beth reached for Will's hand and Ivy saw the way his fingers twined with Beth's, as if he was acutely aware of each place where their hands touched. Ivy knew that Will loved Beth as deeply as Ivy did. But had something changed—was he *in* love?

Will pulled back suddenly. Beth bit her lip, then tucked her hand beneath her leg. Ivy wished she had been more discreet in her staring. Trying to steer them onto a light topic, she said, "You're back just in time, Beth. Philip, Mom, and Andrew are coming to the Cape Sunday. You guys better get cracking on *The Angel and the Alley Cat.*"

It was a graphic novel, a series of adventures that Will and Beth had created for Philip.

"I've got a zillion ideas," Beth said. "I just hope my illustrator can keep up with me."

Will laughed.

"But first Will's going to teach me how to stand-up paddleboard," Beth said to Ivy. "Do you think I can get my hair to spike like that?"

Will self-consciously brushed down his damp hair, and Ivy sat back, smiling to herself.

"Ivy," Beth said, her face growing serious, "what's

going on with Luke? Will told me what happened Saturday night."

What Bryan claimed to have happened, Ivy silently corrected her friend.

She didn't want to endanger Will and Beth by revealing that Bryan was the murderer—the kind who killed those who knew what he had done. But it was time to tell them about Tristan's return; she and Tristan might need their help.

"Luke isn't who Bryan thinks he is."

Will and Beth looked at her, puzzled.

"The real Luke died. He drowned off Chatham."

"Drowned!" Will exclaimed. "Then who is—"

"Tristan. It's Luke's body, but Tristan's spirit."

A small gasp escaped Beth.

"Tristan's occupying Luke?" Will asked. As Ivy explained everything, Will gazed out at the ocean, his eyes darting over the vast blue, as if he was seeing anew the reel of events from the last five weeks.

"It's no more unbelievable than Gregory possessing me," Beth remarked quietly.

"There is one difference," Ivy told her. "Tristan has taken on all of Luke's body. Luke's spirit—his mind, his memories, his soul—is gone. He died and went on."

"Does Gregory know that Tristan has returned?" Beth asked.

"Not yet. Not as far as we can tell."

Will frowned. "Where's Gregory now?"

"I don't know."

"He'll be back," Beth said. "He wants revenge."

They sat silently. Beth's cell phone rang, and she automatically shut it off.

"It's your mom," Ivy and Will said at the same time, recognizing the ringtone.

Beth read the text, then pulled the car keys out of her pocket. "Be back in a minute."

When she had disappeared, Will turned to Ivy. "I'm really sorry, Ivy. I didn't understand what was happening when Tristan first came back. I felt like you had just thrown me aside."

"After all you had done for me!" Her voice shook a little.

Will leaned forward, making her look at him. "I knew you had never stopped loving Tristan. Even when I was most in love with you, I knew you loved him, too. And that was okay with me. I trusted your heart—knew it was large enough to love us both. Then when this stranger came between us, I couldn't understand. I was so angry—at you and at myself."

"I'm sorry, Will, for all the pain I've caused you."

"I thought that I had been duped—like I really didn't know you, like I had fallen for someone who didn't really exist. But the Ivy I knew is back now." He smiled. "You didn't change after all."

Ivy felt a lump in her throat. "Friends?"

He took her hand in his, then lay his other hand on top. "Friends happily everafter."

LATER THAT DAY, WITH AUNT CINDY AND BETH'S mother headed to Provincetown and herself assigned to preparing late afternoon refreshments for guests, Ivy had the perfect opportunity to copy the key to the Steadmans' house. Alone in the kitchen, she lifted it from the pegboard.

"Hey, Ivy."

She quickly turned around, shoving the key into her back pocket.

"Hey, Kels. Dhanya," she answered as they entered the kitchen, surprised that they were still hanging around. "What's up?"

Kelsey flopped in a kitchen chair. *"Bore-dom.* I am totally, horribly bored!"

Observing the tins and plates Ivy had laid out on the kitchen island, Dhanya opened them and began arranging the tea cookies. "There's a seventy percent chance of storms, but Kelsey doesn't want to shop," she said with a shrug.

"Where's Bryan?" Ivy asked.

"He went back to the rink—has to work this afternoon

and tonight. His uncle pushes him too hard," Kelsey complained. "He's always working."

"Or saying he has to," Dhanya suggested quietly.

Kelsey reached for a cookie. "I'd know if he was cheating."

"Want to go shopping, Ivy?" Dhanya asked.

But an idea was forming in Ivy's mind. "What if we surprise Bryan?" she proposed. "Why don't we go skating this evening?"

Ivy figured that, juggling both his job and Kelsey, Bryan would be kept busy and she'd have an opportunity to check out the photographs hanging at the rink for a glimpse of the cufflink.

"Now, that's an idea!" Kelsey said

"Mind if I invite Chase?" Dhanya asked.

"We should invite everybody," Ivy replied. The more distractions for Bryan, the easier her sleuthing job would be. "Make it a party," she advised Kelsey. "You don't want him to think you're desperate to see him."

Kelsey grinned. "Really, Ivy, you know more about dating than you let on."

When tea was over Ivy drove to a shopping area, where she made a copy of the key to the Steadmans' house, then purchased with cash two no-contract phones. With the GPS turned off and no account traceable, communication between her and Tristan would be more secure.

Just before eight, Chase picked up Dhanya and Kelsey, and Will and Beth rode with Ivy to the rink. Max caught up with them in the parking lot. Bryan saw them as soon as they walked through the entrance. "Hey! What a nice surprise!"

"We would have invited you," Kelsey told him, "but you were working."

He gave her a bemused smile. Kelsey, dressed in skin-tight biking shorts and a workout top with a plunging neckline, was obviously asking for attention.

"It was Ivy's idea," she added.

Bryan's smile faded. "Really," he said to Ivy. "I didn't realize you were a big fan of skating."

"I'm sure I told you—last winter Beth and I skated every weekend."

His eyes narrowed ever so slightly; he was suspicious and would be watching her.

"Beats jogging," Beth added.

He flashed Beth a smile. "Beth, glad you're back! In your honor, free passes!" He went to the counter and grabbed tickets for all of them, including other skaters who were entering at the same time, making a show of it.

Beth blushed.

"Come on, everybody, get your skates." He herded them to the rental desk, back in his old role of boisterous camp counselor, the kind of guy liked by team members, little hockey campers, parents, frat brothers. . . .

To Ivy, Bryan was more frightening than Gregory, when Gregory was alive. Her stepbrother had never pretended to like anyone but a chosen few. Bryan was everybody's pal, and could turn on you without notice.

"Hey, Chase, you've got your manly look going tonight!" Bryan teased as they exchanged their shoes and sandals for skates.

Will grinned, but Chase didn't appear to appreciate the remark, despite the fact that his ruggedly handsome look—unshaven face plus uncombed head of dark curls—must have been deliberate. He was hanging back with Dhanya, and looked as if he had come only because she had wanted him to.

Max, who owned his skates and was sitting on a bench lacing them, looked up. Ivy caught the wistful look on his face as he watched Dhanya smile and touch Chase's rough cheek.

Max's slight build and monochrome coloring—light brown hair, light brown eyes, and year-round tan—made him the physical antithesis of Chase. But, as always, Ivy found attractive the people she liked and had begun to see the appeal in his boyish smile and the intriguing, almost amber depths of his eyes.

"Maxie, you've got your usual look going," Bryan joked.

Max responded with a shrug and a smile. Ivy wondered

if Max had any idea what his good friend was capable of. *No way,* she thought.

Her rental skates laced, she stood up, eager to get to the hallway leading to the rink. She remembered from their last time here that there were photos on the walls of the passageway as well as in the snack bar. But she remained where she was, shifting her weight from skate to skate, not wanting Bryan to notice her perusing the photos.

While the others were still lacing up, Bryan's uncle emerged from the hallway.

"Hey, looks like the party's at my house tonight!" he said in the same loud, laughing voice as his nephew. "Grab your skates, Bryan. You've earned it."

Bryan gave his uncle a salute and headed off. As soon as he and Uncle Pat were out of sight, Ivy started toward the hallway.

Most of the photos were of teams, rows of identical-looking kids in hockey helmets, with the team name and year printed at the bottom. But there were a few additional pictures. She recognized Uncle Pat, receiving some kind of award, standing in front of a banner that said CHAMBER OF COMMERCE. There was a black-and-white photo of him with a young Ted Kennedy, and a color one with Mitt Romney.

"Well, I'm impressed," Chase said sarcastically, joining Ivy at the wall of pictures.

Ivy pointed. "Who's that?"

"Tom Brady. Patriots quarterback."

"And this guy?"

"Wayne Gretzky, I think. Hockey megastar."

Dhanya walked toward them. "Wow," she said. "Bryan's uncle is friends with a lot of famous people!"

"He's been *photographed* with them," Chase corrected.

"Hey, what's everybody looking at?" Bryan had returned, skates in hand.

"Your family's fabulous connections," Chase said.

Bryan laughed. "That's my uncle for you, hanging out with the rich and powerful. Actually, he's done a lot of fund-raisers for the community."

As the group moved on, Ivy hung back, her eyes drawn to a photo at the end of the hall. Two kids, seven or eight years old, wearing oversize hockey shirts and Santa caps, stood on ice skates, grinning at the camera, their arms around each other. Little Bryan and Luke, long ago, probably during a Christmas vacation.

"Recognize him?" Bryan's voice sounded close to her ear.

Ivy glanced sideways. The others had gone on. "How could you have turned on your best friend?"

"Easy," Bryan said. "Luke wasn't going anywhere. But I was, Ivy, and still am. Tragic, isn't it?" he added, then laughed in the same deceptively easygoing way he had laughed about his uncle's connections. It chilled her to the heart.

"Want to be my skating partner?" he asked.

"You've got one waiting," she replied, with a nod toward Kelsey, who had turned back, looking for Bryan.

"Oh. Her." He smiled at Ivy, then moved on.

Ivy reluctantly followed, promising herself she'd return to the photos as soon as she could sneak away. For a while she skated with Max. Each time she banked the curve at one end of the oblong rink, she stole a glance at the snack bar, wishing her friends would quickly get thirsty so she'd have an excuse to check out the photos. There were dividers between the concessions and the risers that surrounded the rink, but the food area was still visible, and Bryan would be watching if she left the ice alone.

At the moment, he was skating with Kelsey and a little girl. The child, wearing a hockey camp T-shirt and helmet, her braids flying behind her, was grinning from ear to ear.

Max followed Ivy's eyes. "The kids love Bryan. He's a great coach. My dad says he'd make a great salesman."

Ivy moved a stride ahead of Max and turned to skate backward, facing him. In her search for someone who may have seen something without realizing its importance, Max was a good place to begin. "When did you guys first become friends?" she asked.

"In college."

"Not till then?"

"It was during hockey season, actually, a party after a big game. It kind of surprised me that Bryan would hang with me—you know, him being a star on campus."

It didn't surprise Ivy. Bryan would like a rich friend with expensive toys—like a boat.

Max smiled. "Then when we found out he was working just ten miles from my house every summer, it was awesome!"

Ivy nodded. "I guess so! You liked the beach. You both were boaters." She continued to skate backward, observing Max's face.

"Well, Bryan didn't know much about boating, but he really liked it."

"Yeah?" Ivy said. Max allowed Bryan to drive his cars. Would he hand over the key to a boat? Probably.

"We started coming down weekends in May to putter around."

At what point, Ivy wondered, had Bryan formed his plan to kill Luke and dump him in the ocean? And how successful had he been at washing away every bit of evidence? Maybe, if he was in a hurry—

Ivy saw Bryan coming up behind Max, staring hard at her. She turned to skate side by side with Max, so their conversation wouldn't look like an interrogation.

"Would you take me out in your boat?" she asked.

"Sure. Which one?"

She hesitated. "The powerboat."

"That'd be great."

They skated a few more loops together, then Ivy saw Dhanya and Chase leave the ice, and hurried to join them. "Hey, guys." She dropped down on the lowest bench of the riser. "Hungry?"

Dhanya glanced at Chase. "Maybe food would help. . . . He's not feeling so good," she told Ivy. "The lights are bothering him."

Ivy glanced up at the rink lights, then studied Chase's face.

He shielded his eyes with his hand. "Maybe food would help, if it's not all-American greasy stuff."

"I doubt it's tofu and green tea, but there might be something plain, like a soft pretzel," Ivy said, and led the way.

The concession area had wooden tables and chairs painted in bright orange and blue, a cheerful contrast to the warehouse gray of the rink. The mosaic of framed photos, hanging on facing walls, began with black-and-white and changed over to color. While Dhanya and Chase surveyed his options, Ivy checked out the pictures, starting with what appeared to be the most recent ones. In addition to the posed team pictures, there were action shots, and Ivy recognized Bryan in several of them in which he appeared to be teaching younger players.

Her heart skipped a beat: Bryan in a sport coat. She pushed a chair out of the way to get closer to the photo.

No use—she couldn't see his shirt cuff. It looked like a ceremony in which he and his uncle were giving out trophies to kids.

There was another photo of Bryan and Luke, which must have been taken in high school. Ivy swallowed hard. It was strange to see a face she now thought of as Tristan's staring back at her, looking like a relaxed and cocky hockey player.

"Are you stuck on him or me?" Bryan asked in a quiet voice.

Ivy jumped. "Him, of course. When was this taken?"

"Senior year, just before we won the city championship. Just before Luke dropped out of school."

"Did he? That's too bad," Ivy said.

"Less than three months till graduation, and Luke dropped out. He didn't care about anything except hockey and Corinne—and me," Bryan added, grinning. "Luke cared about me."

Ivy wanted to slap him. She hated Bryan's reckless indifference. And she was afraid of it. There was no appealing for fairness, much less mercy, when a person was devoid of feelings for others.

To Ivy's relief, Kelsey was coming toward them with two tall cones, and Will and Beth had just taken a break.

After excusing herself, Ivy joined them for ice cream, then returned to the rink.

"C'mon, Ivy. Like we used to," Beth invited her. They moved around the ice arm in arm, in perfect rhythm, as they had last winter. Beth sang with the canned music; Ivy provided harmony.

As they skated, Ivy kept looking around, trying to figure out the layout of the building. She saw signs for the men's and women's lockers and doors to other rooms that appeared to be used for maintenance and storage. Somewhere Uncle Pat had to have an office. It was her last hope for an incriminating picture: a shrine of family photos.

Will joined them, and they skated three across with Ivy in the middle. After several laps, Ivy let go of their hands. "Catch up with you later," she said. When the two of them didn't close the gap between them, Ivy put Beth's hand in Will's, then skated off.

Uncle Pat had put on his "date music," and out of the corner of her eye, Ivy had seen Bryan and Kelsey step onto the ice at the far end of the rink. Ivy made a beeline for the locker room. Inside a bathroom stall, she undid one skate, then slipped its lace under the blade of her other, rubbing back and forth until it broke. Now she had an excuse for padding around in her socks and, if necessary, pretending to be lost on her way to the rental desk. Between the food and lobby areas, she found the door she wanted, one with a plaque that read PATRICK CAVANAUGH, OWNER, MANAGER, THE BOSS, AND DON'T YOU FORGET IT!

The office was lit and the door partway open. She listened intently for a moment, then nudged it. There was no response from within. After peeking around the door, she slipped inside.

Just as she had hoped! Sports photos, family photos, and framed clippings from newspapers.

"Looking for something?"

Ivy froze, then turned slowly to face Bryan.

"Oh! Mr. Cavanaugh!"

"That's what it says on the door."

Ivy nodded. "You sound just like Bryan. I'm Ivy, a friend of Bryan's."

"Is there a problem?"

Ivy held up the skates and the broken lace.

He raised an eyebrow. "The rental shop's that way," he said, pointing.

"I know." Ivy had grown alarmingly good at lying, and one of the tricks she had learned was to tell as much truth as possible in a lie. "I shouldn't have come in, but I wanted to look at your photographs. I saw some in the snack bar. You have a few really good ones of Bryan coaching."

The man smiled. She had hit the target, an uncle's extreme pride in his talented nephew. "He's great with

43

those kids. He could make a living coaching, if he wasn't so damn good at it himself."

"Bryan said his mom was a player."

Uncle Pat chuckled. "Yeah, I bet he told you she was better than me and my brothers."

"Was she?"

"Yeah." His laughter boomed. "Here she is," he said, pointing to a photo, which allowed Ivy to move farther into the room.

Ivy grinned: sturdily built, Bryan's mother looked like him with a ribbon in his hair. Next to her photo was a newspaper clipping, yellowed with age, the photo showing a much younger, slimmer Uncle Pat, and the headline announcing ANOTHER CAVANAUGH LEADS TEAM TO CHAMPIONSHIP. Buying time, Ivy stopped to read the article, and when she heard Bryan's uncle move toward his desk, she quickly shifted her eyes to scan the wall of photos. There it was! A picture of Bryan in a tux, accepting a trophy. From where she stood, she couldn't see enough to tell if a cufflink was showing. She dragged her eyes back to the old article about Uncle Pat.

"It's kind of awesome," she said, "to hand down a sport in a family. It says in this article your dad was a great goalie. Is he still around to see Bryan play?"

"No, but he saw him as a youngster. You kind of interested in Bryan?"

Uncle Pat had just handed her the excuse she needed.

She forced herself to gush. "I'd love to see him play!"

"Bryan gets tickets from the university for the home games. You should ask him."

"Maybe I will," Ivy said, feigning a shy smile. She moved along the wall toward her goal. "That's a good picture of him. What award is he getting?" She peered closely at the photo. With his elbows bent and his hands grasping the trophy, Bryan's cufflink was clearly visible. When enlarged, would it provide sufficient evidence? She almost gasped when she saw the familiar date written on the photo's mat: the day of the hit-and-run.

"He was a finalist in the Northeast Interscholastic Athletic Association."

NIAA, Ivy said to herself over and over, memorizing it.

"To get that far he had to be voted Providence's High School Player of the Year—not just among hockey players, but all athletes."

"Awesome!" She read the white script in the bottom corner of the photo: *D. L. Pabst,* she repeated to herself— the professional photographer, the person who would have the electronic file.

"There must be a lot of pressure on Bryan."

"Well, if anybody can handle it, he can." Uncle Pat looked at her thoughtfully. "You know, you should really be having this conversation with Bryan. Most guys are flattered by a pretty girl's interest."

Ivy tried to look sweet and wistful. "The thing is, he's my roommate's boyfriend. Please—please, don't tell him I asked about him."

Uncle Pat winked. "Your secret's safe with me."

"Thanks for the photo tour."

"Sure. Anytime."

She turned to leave.

"Ivy," he called after her.

"Yes?"

"Bryan never stays with one girl too long. You'll have your chance."

My chance to put him behind bars, she thought. "Thanks. I hope so!"

Four

JAGGED LIGHTNING SCISSORED THE MIDNIGHT SKY
and thunder cracked. Tristan pressed Ivy against him,
although he knew his instinct was pointless—his body
couldn't shield hers from a lightning strike.

"One more house," Ivy shouted as the needles of rain
became a downpour.

They ran the last forty yards to the Steadmans' front
door, Tristan sprinting ahead, pulling Ivy with him.
Another streak of lightning struck closer and was followed
instantly by an earsplitting clap. Tristan held the flashlight

while Ivy slipped the key into the lock. They rushed inside, then he slammed the door behind them, shutting out the storm.

Ivy touched his arm. "Tristan, you're shaking."

He dropped his heavy backpack with a thud. He wanted to yell at her for paddling to him on the open water when storms were predicted. "Gregory struck once, Ivy. He'll strike again!"

"We're safe now," she said, putting her arms around him.

She was soaked to the bone, and while he knew how strong her spirit was, her body felt fragile to him. He shut his eyes. If only he could be the lightning rod, he thought, and draw Gregory's vengeance away from her.

"Everything's okay, Tristan."

But it wasn't. It had been almost a week since Gregory had left Beth. He was planning something—another deadly strike, another possession of someone's mind.

"I've got some good news," Ivy said, linking her hands around his neck and leaning back a little, sounding pleased with herself. "I found the photo!"

She recounted her evening at the ice rink. "I can call the photographer and order a copy."

"And then?" Tristan asked.

"Take it to the police. They should be able to subpoena the electronic file and enlarge it enough to get a good image."

He shook his head. She wasn't thinking things through. "Even if they do, Ivy, it doesn't prove Bryan had a motive to kill *Corinne*. We still need evidence that she was black-mailing him about this incident. And if the police don't make an immediate arrest—"

"One step at a time," she interrupted. "I'll find that evidence too."

He pulled her close again, burying his face in her wet hair.

"Come on," she said softly. "Let's explore."

The ground floor had a foyer and a large family room to the right with glass doors at the back, which Tristan assumed faced Nauset Harbor. To the left and six steps up from the foyer was a living-dining area and kitchen. Flashes from the storm illuminated long windows, as well as skylights in the cathedral ceiling. A large contemporary fireplace occupied the far wall. Tristan followed Ivy in a circle of the first floor and up another half flight of steps to the bedrooms. The huge master bedroom also had skylights. The two smaller rooms appeared to be children's rooms.

"I don't know if I'll be able to sleep here," Tristan said, trying to make a joke. "I kind of like places with strong fishy smells and bird droppings."

"You'll get used to it," Ivy replied, her smile lit by a pale halo from the penlight she carried, then suddenly bleached by a flash of lightning.

"Stay with me tonight," Tristan pleaded. "At least until the storms are over."

She brushed his cheek with the backs of her fingers. "For a few hours. I have to be back at the cottage before the others are up."

As tired as they both were, it seemed strange to move into someone's house uninvited and sleep in their beds, so they carried blankets and pillows to the living room and spread them on the floor. Ivy set the alarm on her iPhone and fell asleep immediately. Tristan held her in his arms, listening to her soft breathing. The rain stopped, the thunder became a distant rumble, and Tristan drifted off.

He was awakened by a keening sound. Sitting up quickly, Tristan turned toward the foyer. A flicker of blue light played across the surface of the front door. Ivy stirred, opening her eyes, and Tristan placed one finger over her lips.

What? she mouthed.

"Stay here," he whispered, knowing she probably wouldn't.

He tiptoed to the top of the short flight of steps and saw a shifting blue light on the foyer's ceramic tiles. The TV was on, its sound muted. Tristan crept down the steps. He felt Ivy next to him as he peered into the family room. On the large screen a grotesque mouth opened wider and wider, the camera moving in for a close-up of what must have been a bloodcurdling scream.

Swiftly scanning the room, Tristan saw a distinct purple mist curled like a cat in one corner of a sofa. "Lacey?"

"Oh," said the purple mist. "Did I wake you guys?"

Tristan heard Ivy laughing in relief.

"What are you doing here?" Tristan asked.

"Watching a video. Since you're awake, I may as well turn it up." She slowly materialized on the sofa and picked up the remote.

Tristan glanced toward the double doors, then the windows. "Lacey, it's the middle of the night, and we don't want to call attention to ourselves."

"I checked the shades. They're tight." She propped her booted feet on the coffee table in front of her. "Do you know this movie? Sit down. You'll love it!"

"That's you, isn't it?" Ivy asked, pointing toward the screen.

"This was my first film," Lacey boasted. "When I auditioned, the producer said to the director, 'We're not going to find a mouth that big on any other nine-year-old.'"

For a moment Tristan watched a young Lacey run for her life from what appeared to be a scaly roach on steroids. Out of the corner of his eye, he saw Ivy check the time on her phone, then sit down on the other end of the sofa to watch.

"I didn't think horror flicks would be your thing," Lacey said to Ivy, sounding pleased.

"Not usually, but you're in it."

Lacey was running through a primeval forest, looks of panic and fear just about exploding off her face. Apparently, subtlety wasn't her style.

"What do you think?" she asked.

"Very . . . dramatic," Ivy replied.

Tristan sat on a chair near the sofa. "Would you turn that off a minute so we can talk?"

"I can talk over it," Lacey assured him.

"I can't."

The angel watched a moment longer, then hit Pause. A large image of her terror-struck face hung frozen on the screen.

"Lacey, we haven't seen any sign of Gregory. Do you know what's going on?"

"No, but I can guess."

"So guess," Tristan told her.

"His lightning stunt knocked him out for a bit. But you know the old saying—if it doesn't kill you, it'll make you stronger. He's probably out there cruising now, looking for a new mind to take over."

"Even though he was more potent as a bolt of lightning?" Tristan asked.

"That's only if you equate power with frying people," Lacey replied. "Gregory has always loved having power in social situations, manipulating people and watching them do what he wants. That's how he was alive; that's how he is dead." She sighed. "It's a common problem for us dead folks—we're too used to having a body.

"I don't need hands to move things"—the TV remote spun on the coffee table, then Lacey reached out with a materialized hand and stopped it—"but I like to have them. Thinking and acting like a human, it's a real hard habit to kick. Gregory will take over another mind, a more agreeable one than Beth's, and get himself a good set of hands. I guarantee it."

"I have to stop him," Tristan said.

"No," Lacey replied, "Ivy does. *Bryan* is your enemy. It's Bryan who's most likely to cut short your time to redeem yourself. Gregory doesn't even know you're around. He becomes your enemy only if you allow him to."

"He became my enemy the first time he tried to kill Ivy."

"And look where that landed you—in a cemetery!"

Tristan saw Ivy flinch.

"I'm sorry to have to remind you," Lacey went on, "but you are no longer Ivy's angel. You've got your own battle now."

Tristan ignored her. "Gregory tried to kill Ivy through Beth. Before that, he tried on Morris Island, and—"

"To be perfectly accurate," Lacey interrupted, "a car ran Ivy off the island road."

"Gregory was behind the accident, he must have been!"

"Not all the evil in this world can be traced back to Gregory. Your love for Ivy is blinding you."

"Please, Tristan, listen to her," Ivy begged.

"I'll listen when she tells me something useful, like Gregory's M.O.—what he has done, what he's doing now, what he plans to do."

As it was in the beginning, is now, and shall be ever-after. Ours.

Tristan turned his head at the sound of the murmured words, then glanced at the horrified face that hung frozen on the TV screen. Had the voices found him here?

Ivy put her arms around him. "Let me search for those answers, okay? Give me some time, Tristan, and I'll find out everything we need to know."

Her phone alarm sounded. "I have to go."

Tristan started toward the door with her.

"Stay inside," Ivy told him. "Stay safe. Please."

"Just for a second."

He closed the door behind them and walked her as far as the gravel path. "Ivy," he said, resting his hands on her shoulders. "We can spin a million theories about my redemption, but this much we know: Love is good. There's no way that my loving you can damn me."

She was quiet for a moment. "Maybe it's not as simple as one person loving another."

"What do you mean?"

"Maybe it's how we love," she said, "the choices we make."

He was growing irritated. "I don't understand."

"Maybe it's the actions we take, what we *do* when we love."

"Here's what I do," he replied, then kissed her good-bye with the same mix of desire and wonder he had felt the night of the accident on Morris Island.

IVY WAS GLAD IT WAS BETH, KELSEY, AND WILL'S DAY to work breakfast: She would have been too tempted to sit down with one of the guests for a cup of coffee. Not that it wasn't tempting to climb into one of the beds she was changing.

When her job was done, she went to the beach, planning to catch up on her sleep. She set her towel down several hundred feet from the handful of sunbathers. With the dunes far behind her, and the rooflines of the inn and private homes a receding horizon above the shrub-covered bluffs, she happily wriggled her toes in the warm grains of sand, then rolled over onto her stomach.

Beth was back at the cottage, typing up a storm, making up for lost time after Gregory had blocked her ability to write. Ivy hoped that she and Will would get together to work on their graphic novel—for their sake, not Philip's. That was her last thought before falling asleep.

Sometime later, Dhanya's voice woke her up: "Why are you way over here?"

Ivy opened one eye. "Just wanted to be away from our guests."

Dhanya kicked off her flip-flops and spread out her towel. "I almost didn't see you."

I almost pulled it off, Ivy thought, then shut her eyes.

Listening to the whispery flick of pages as Dhanya read her paperback, Ivy drifted back into the lovely whiteness of a beach doze. The grind of sandy footsteps headed in their direction brought her back to consciousness.

"Kelsey told me to look for you." The sound of Bryan's voice sent light prickles up Ivy's arms. "If you had walked any farther, we'd be in Chatham."

"Ivy wanted to be away from people," Dhanya explained.

"But not from me," Bryan said as he laid his towel next to Ivy's.

Ivy took her time turning over. "Certainly not from *friends*. Where's Kels?"

"Looking for her sunglasses. Did you have fun at the rink last night?" Bryan's tone was casual, but his eyes were so attentive, Ivy felt as if he was somehow taking her temperature.

"Yeah, it's fun doing a winter sport in the middle of summer."

"Then we should do it again soon," Bryan said. "Did you guys hear about Max's party tomorrow night?"

"I talked Chase into going," Dhanya replied.

"And Beth, Will, and me," Ivy said, though it wasn't Dhanya's persuasion that had made up her mind. Ivy had realized that it was the perfect opportunity to revisit the scene of the crime, to understand what happened the night Bryan left the party and murdered Luke. Figuring out Bryan's track, she'd know where else to look for evidence against him.

Bryan shot her a mocking smile. "Well, what d'ya know. Max will be happy that you're finally accepting one of his invitations."

"Guess it's time to see what I'm missing. Hey, here comes Kels." Ivy waved her down.

"What is this, a camping trip?" Kelsey complained as she dropped her pile of stuff on the other side of Bryan. She was sporting a sleek pair of sunglasses.

Bryan glanced over his shoulder. "Those look like my driving glasses."

"They are," Kelsey replied. "I must have left mine at Max's. Look what else I found in your car," she added in a coy voice.

After another backward glance, Bryan wrenched around on his towel. Kelsey moved her arm up and away from Bryan, teasing him. "Found it in your backseat."

The small object flashed with sunlight, then Ivy got a clear view of the hair fastener, a distinctive triangle with purple wampum beads. She went cold all over. It was Alicia's—she was wearing it the first time Ivy met her. And she must have been wearing it the night Bryan killed her.

"I'll take that," Bryan said calmly, having recovered from the initial shock.

"Whose is it?' Kelsey asked, holding it behind her back.

"Come on, Kelsey, give it over," he said, stretching out his hand, palm up. "It's not yours."

"No kidding!" she replied, pulling it out to look at it again, then slipping it into her hair. "It belongs to some girl you were fooling around with in the backseat."

Ivy cringed at the truth behind Kelsey's words.

"Who is she?" Kelsey demanded. As Bryan reached for her, she rose to her knees. Bryan grabbed a fistful of her hair, but she was quick, removing the clasp before he could.

"Stop making a scene," he said. "At school I drive a zillion people around."

Ivy's mind raced. Another piece of evidence. Alicia's family would identify it. A strand of hair might be caught in it. And Dhanya and Ivy both had heard Kelsey say where it was found—

"Keep away!" Kelsey cried. "Heads up, Ivy!" She tossed it to her.

Bryan spun around. His eyes met Ivy's, the determination in them burning like a dark fire. He'd break her fingers if he had to. But she curled her hand all the tighter around the clasp. She suspected it was Alicia's favorite, maybe given to her by someone she loved—maybe Luke. Ivy couldn't let go.

Bryan moved slowly toward her, his eyes pinned to Ivy, never blinking. She took a step back, then another.

"Throw it to me," Kelsey called, thinking it all a game. "Throw it to me again!"

But Ivy held it behind her back. As Bryan advanced, she knew she didn't have a chance—she'd lose a race to the inn—but she was beyond logical thinking. She gripped it as if she could protect this one thing precious to Alicia, and took off.

Bryan must not have expected it. For a moment he stood flat-footed. Then he moved with the speed of an animal predator, catching her easily, holding her tightly against him.

Kelsey was on them ten seconds later, her laughter replaced with anger. "You can't control yourself, can you, Ivy? You just can't keep from flirting."

"I know who this belongs to. I'm going to return it to her."

"Who?" Kelsey asked. "Who's he been seeing?"

"A girl who trusted too much."

"It's yours, isn't it?" Kelsey accused Ivy. "That's why you've been sneaking out at night."

"What?!"

Bryan relaxed his bruising grip, a sardonic smile lighting his face. "Sneaking around, Ivy? Visiting anyone I know?"

"Kelsey, have you ever seen me wear this?" Ivy demanded. "Have you ever seen anything like this on my bureau or in my jewelry box?"

Kelsey went through everyone's bureaus, as readily as she went through Bryan's car, to see if there was something she wanted to borrow. She thought for a moment. "I—I guess not." She turned to him with a conspiratorial smile. "On the count of three: I'll tickle, you grab."

Bryan threw Ivy to the ground so fast it knocked her breath away. Kelsey tickled, but it was the strength of his fingers that pried free the clasp. Ivy bit his hand. For a second he let go, and Kelsey snatched it up.

She ran off, holding it in the air like a trophy, glancing behind her to make sure Bryan was following. He chased her and swept her off her feet. Ivy watched Kelsey laughing and screaming as he flung her over his back and carried her toward the water. She shouted and kicked her feet, but he was strong enough to carry her straight through the breakers. Turning for a moment to gaze at Ivy, he laughed.

Ivy felt like she was going to throw up, watching him make a joke of dragging someone else into deep water. When she saw Bryan's arm hurl an object into even deeper ocean, she knew it was the clasp.

He and Kelsey swam back to a depth where they could stand. He pulled her to him in a passionate kiss.

Hands shaking, Ivy gathered together her things.

Dhanya, who had been watching the show in the surf, turned to her with a look of surprise. "Leaving already? Ivy, you're not really interested in Bryan, are you?"

"No." Her anger and frustration made her voice sound clipped. Ivy forced herself to speak more slowly. "Bryan's definitely not my type."

"Didn't think so. But he *is* the cheating type," Dhanya remarked. "Do you know who the fastener belonged to?"

Ivy shook her head. "I was just yanking his chain," she said, and began the long trudge across the sand.

Dhanya and anyone else who had been watching the charade would have seen nothing but Bryan playing a dating game. Ivy saw a murderer who didn't mind ripping people's hearts out, then tossing them like broken shells into the sea.

Five

WHEN IVY, WILL, AND BETH ARRIVED AT THE PARTY Saturday night, it was in full swing. Ivy could barely squeeze her VW onto Max's front lawn. She had offered to drive that evening, and Beth had quickly chosen the front seat. Perhaps she'd sensed Ivy's need to follow the same route as they had the night of their accident and drive past the spot without getting spooked.

Now, with the first challenge on her list checked off successfully, Ivy walked with her friends around the side of the

Moyers' house, following the blazing tiki lamps and the pulsing music of the party. Will whistled with soft amazement as he took in the place and its panoramic view. Max's waterfront home was an elongated rectangle. With upper and lower decks running the length of the building, and its white rails and round lights, it reminded Ivy of a cruise ship run aground. But the thing Ivy had most hoped to see was missing.

"There's no dock."

"Well, aren't we being picky!" Will teased.

Following Will and Beth, Ivy climbed a set of exterior steps up to the lower deck. The party was spread across it and filled the rooms that faced it. Leaving Will and Beth playing ping-pong in the first room, which also had billiards and a Wii, Ivy wove through the crowd to the deck again. On a night like this, she thought, Bryan had slipped off to murder Luke.

"Ivy! You came!" Max called to her from his perch on the railing ten feet away. "I was afraid you'd changed your mind."

She smiled and joined him.

"Did you try some of the games?" he asked. "There's an electronic and pinball arcade in the next room. And a 3-D movie showing in the theater, next to the kitchen."

"Actually, I wanted to walk down to your beach," Ivy told him.

At the moment only two small boats were moored off-shore, bobbing in the moonlight. Where was the rest of Max's fleet?

"Want company?" Max leaped lightly to the deck. After snagging two sodas, they walked in a comfortable silence along a wood-chip path. The Moyers' land eased down to the sea, and partygoers were scattered across a series of landscaped terraces.

If Bryan had left with Luke from here, wouldn't there be witnesses? Ivy thought. Two people leaving and just one coming back—someone had to have noticed.

"So those boats are yours?" she asked aloud.

"The sailboat belongs to a friend of my dad's. We use the little powerboat like a taxi. Our other boats are at the marina by the causeway, where they're better protected."

Protected from more than storms, Ivy thought, disap-pointed. But maybe marinas had security cameras.

"When I take you out, we can use whichever boat you want," he added.

"About how long would it take to sail from the marina to Lighthouse Beach?" she asked.

Max turned to look at her curiously. "That's where you want to go?"

It was where "Luke" had washed ashore. Ivy searched for an excuse. "Aren't there some seals there?"

"More in the winter. But we can go if you want, down

to Monomoy and up along South Beach toward the light-house."

"Great! Is it far? How long would it take to get there, to the lighthouse?"

"Motoring rather than sailing, an hour."

A two-hour round trip for Bryan, she thought. And much longer if she added in the struggle and the disposal of the body, plus the cleanup back at the marina. Wouldn't Max have noticed that his close friend was missing for a long time?

"I'm free Monday," he offered.

"That would be great!"

As they walked the beach, Max told Ivy of the different places he had sailed.

"Do you ever boat after dark?" she asked.

"Sometimes with Bryan. He likes night fishing, but you've got to be really alert when sailing at night."

Ivy figured Bryan had been very alert, watching every-thing Max did to learn how to handle a boat under the cover of darkness.

They started up the path toward the house. Two people sprawled on the lawn called out to Max. "Awesome party!" But a foursome passed them on the path without even look-ing at him.

"Max, do you actually know everybody here?"

He laughed and took a swig of soda. "I don't think half

of them know I'm the guy having the party. Sometimes I get tired of the noise and leave, and they just rock on."

"When Beth and I were in the accident, were you at your party?"

Max's back straightened—the question had caught him off guard. "Yeah. I was around."

"Was Bryan?"

Max glanced about. Looking to see if anyone else was within earshot? Ivy wondered. Perhaps thinking through his response and searching for words that didn't incriminate.

"The police interviewed a lot of people from your party," she went on. "I read the detailed report."

Max's quick blink told her that he believed her fib—he thought she knew who was present during the police investigation. He glanced away. "Bryan wasn't here right then," he confessed.

"With all these guests, how do you know?"

"Because . . . I looked for him."

"So, Bryan also leaves your parties sometimes. Does he borrow your car and ride around? Or your boat?"

Max took his time answering. "I think we'd run out of ice and he went to get it."

Bryan would have been absent from the party a lot longer than it took to get ice, Ivy figured. Was Max ignorant of that or covering for him?

She pushed further: "Did he go by car or boat? I suppose the marina sells ice, so he could have taken your little taxi."

"I don't really remember, Ivy. I—I was drinking a lot that night."

They walked the rest of the way in an uneasy silence. When someone called out to them from a dark bench along the path, Max jumped.

"Hey, Chase," Ivy answered, and heard Max let his breath out slowly. Following Max's eyes to the deck above them, she saw Bryan sitting on the rail, watching them.

Max shifted his weight from foot to foot. "I better check on things."

"Sure. Catch you later," Ivy said, hoping she hadn't put Max in danger. She turned toward Chase.

He was alone, sitting on the bench with his legs sprawling and arms draped over the back, looking looser than she'd ever seen him. Sitting down, Ivy could smell the alcohol—something stronger than beer, she thought. An empty cup was tipped over under the bench; Chase was swirling the contents of a second cup.

"Having a good time?" he asked Ivy, and took a noisy sip. "Who'd you come with tonight?"

"Beth and Will."

"Couldn't get a date?"

Ivy laughed lightly at his assumption. "Didn't want one."

"B'cause you're still pining over . . . what's-his-name," Chase guessed. "The guy who likes to murder his old girlfriends."

Ivy prickled. "If you're referring to Luke, he was *accused* of murdering a former girlfriend."

"*Accused*," Chase echoed mockingly. "Obviously, you're still pining."

"No."

Chase tried to raise an eyebrow, but his sharp good looks had gone mushy with alcohol.

"Luke isn't the person I thought he was."

"Even so," Chase said, "girls like dangerous guys. They get a thrill from trying to tame them."

"Not this girl," Ivy answered.

"Where is he?" His question sounded more like a demand.

"I don't know."

"Where do you *think* he is?" Chase persisted.

Ivy leaned forward and looked into Chase's eyes. "Nowhere nearby, if he has half a brain."

"But nowhere far away," Chase countered. "Not if you sank your hooks into him."

Ivy sat back. "Whatever. I'm leaving that mystery for the police to solve."

"What mystery is that?"

Bryan's deep voice startled Ivy. Crossing the grass

behind them, rather than taking the path, he had probably hoped to rattle her.

"Hey, Bryan," she said as casually as possible.

His hands grasped the back of the bench, and he bent forward, towering over their heads. "So what mystery are you two trying to solve?"

"*Chase* is the one who's trying," she replied.

"Where your old friend is hiding out," Chase said. "What do you think?"

"Luke? He's not my friend anymore."

"I guess not"—Chase grinned—"now that you've ratted on him!"

"He was once a close friend," Bryan continued calmly. "So I don't want to know where he is. I don't want to be tempted to report him."

It chilled Ivy, how sincere Bryan appeared, playing the role of a guy torn between an old friendship and civic responsibility.

"I wonder if there's a reward being offered," Chase said.

Ivy looked up and saw the slight widening of Bryan's eyes. He laid a firm hand on Chase's shoulder. "If I were you, I'd steer clear of it all." The tone of his advice bordered on menacing. "Some people will do anything not to get caught." Then Bryan laughed loudly, and Chase laughed along with him.

"Where's Kelsey?" Ivy asked.

"Who knows?" Bryan replied. "Guzzling down drinks somewhere."

Ivy rose to her feet, glad that Kelsey wasn't clinging to Bryan, but uncomfortable not knowing where she was.

Returning to the house, she scanned the deck and both game rooms, slipped inside the darkened theater, then checked the kitchen. No Kelsey. She exited again through the kitchen's sliding doors. The final illuminated room along the deck was striking. Its glass shelves and black lacquered wood gleamed, the furniture reflecting off a highly polished black-and-white marble floor. An assortment of colored glass on the fireplace mantel drew Ivy's attention, and she didn't see Kelsey at first. Then, spotting her curled low in the corner of a sectional, Ivy quickly slid open the screen.

"You okay?" she asked, hurrying to her. Kelsey's red mane was partly over her face. Ivy brushed it back. "Kelsey, are you okay?"

Kelsey rubbed her temples and squinted up at Ivy.

"A bad headache?" Ivy asked.

Kelsey nodded, shutting her eyes for a moment.

"How's your stomach?"

"Queasy. I think this is what happens to my mother when she gets migraines."

"What did you have to drink?"

"A margarita. *One!* Don't preach."

"Okay. So what can I do?"

"Would you take me home?"

"You *are* sick!" Ivy said, resting her hand gently on Kelsey's shoulder.

She quickly texted Beth, Will, and Dhanya to tell them she was taking Kelsey back and would return later for them. She didn't want them to hitch a ride with Chase or Bryan. Then she helped Kelsey to her feet. "Come on. Let's get out of here."

A shadow in the doorway stopped them. "Where are you going?"

Ivy glanced over her shoulder at Bryan. "Kelsey's not feeling well."

"What a surprise," he responded dryly. He strode across the room to them and roughly turned Kelsey's face toward him. Ivy wanted to shove him away, but she knew better than to take any action that might set off him—or Kelsey.

"You drink too much," he said. "You're out of control."

Kelsey pulled away from him. "But I didn't, not tonight."

"Come on," Ivy said to her roommate. "I'm taking you home."

Bryan placed a restraining hand on Ivy's forearm. "I'll take her."

"I'm headed there anyway," Ivy replied, and removed

his hand. She wasn't about to let him drive off with another girl whom he feared was beyond his control.

Bryan wedged himself between Ivy and her roommate. "Well, Kelsey, if that's what you want," he goaded her. "Kate's here—you remember her, Max's neighbor. And hot little Sophie. I won't be bored."

"I'm sure you won't," Kelsey answered dully.

Bryan shot Ivy a suspicious look, as if she was to blame for his inability to stoke Kelsey's jealousy.

"I don't know where my purse is," Kelsey said to Ivy, looking and sounding helpless.

"No problem," Bryan answered quickly. "Ivy and I will look for it."

Before Ivy could step away, Bryan grabbed her. She could feel the pressure of each finger on her arm as he forced her to walk with him to the hall, then dragged her into the room across it, a home office. He backed her into a filing cabinet.

"We had a deal."

"A deal I've kept," Ivy said.

"Then what's gotten into her?"

Ivy shrugged. "Sometimes people just get sick."

"No, there's more to it." Bryan peered into Ivy's face, his own face so close she could smell the beer he'd consumed.

"Don't blow it now, Bryan. You were pretty smooth with Chase."

"Interfering moron!"

"Don't crack the first time your girlfriend goes moody on you," she said. "I thought you were cooler than that."

Bryan pulled back but kept his eyes locked on hers. "If you're lying, I'll find out."

"I know you will—that's why I don't. Now let me get Kelsey home before she throws up."

Ivy ducked past him and, to her relief, saw Beth and Will hurrying down the hall toward her. At the same time a text came back from Dhanya: CHASE IS ACTING OBNOXIOUS. WAIT FOR ME. GOT K'S PURSE W/ MINE.

The five of them rode home silently. When Dhanya and Beth took Kelsey up to bed, Will lingered on the doorstep to ask Ivy if she was okay, then headed to his room.

Ivy's mind was too full of things to be sorted for her to join the others inside. And she was anxious for her roommates to go to bed so she could slip away to Tristan's. She sat on the swing for a few minutes, rocking back and forth, then pushed off from the bench and walked the path through the inn's large garden. Tonight, in the moonlight, the yard was a shimmering silk screen in black and white.

The cottage door opened and Beth emerged.

"How's Kelsey?"

"Not great, but not getting any worse."

Beth joined her in the center of the garden. "Ivy," she

said, "when Gregory was taking over my mind, I had head-aches like that."

Ivy nodded. "And Chase had the same kind two nights ago at the ice rink."

"You think it's Gregory trying out different hosts?"

"I don't know." With one finger, Ivy riffled the deli-cate blossoms of a tall cleome. "I'm surprised that Gregory would try to possess either of them, when there are easier targets available."

"Like Dhanya or Max," Beth said. "I've been wondering about that too. I can't get a good read of Max—there's some-thing about the way he looks at me. . . ." Beth shrugged. "But I think, for Gregory's purposes, Dhanya may be too easy a host. She's susceptible to anyone who tells her what to do, which makes it hard if you want to be the only person calling the shots. And Gregory does."

"I never thought of it that way."

They continued along the path through the garden. "Chase may not seem like an ideal candidate, and he would fight Gregory at first," Beth conceded. "But Chase is needy and ambitious. Needy people are always vulnerable to others. And ambitious people can be seduced, because they want something they don't have."

"Gregory would know how to play that combination," Ivy agreed quietly.

Reaching the inn, they circled around the edge of the

garden. Beth stopped at the trellis of moonflowers, reaching with her hand to cup a fragrant blossom. Ivy knew the vine was Beth's favorite, for the poetic reason that its large white flowers began to bloom at dusk, when the rest of the garden was fading.

Beth leaned close to Ivy and lowered her voice. "Tristan's nearby, isn't he." It was spoken as a statement rather than a question. "And you have some reason for not telling Will and me where."

Ivy debated once more what was best for them. "Knowledge is dangerous, Beth."

"But we can help you," she insisted, "if you would only let us."

Ivy shook her head. "Not yet. I know you'll be there for me the moment I ask." Ivy hoped she would never have to ask; her friends had been through enough.

"Will and I were talking about you tonight," Beth said. "We want you to wear my amethyst. It helped me; maybe it will help you." She reached back with one hand and slid the delicate chain until she caught the fastener, then unlatched it. "Turn around."

Ivy did and felt the small weight of the pendant against her chest. Her eyes pricked with unexpected tears. Will and Ivy's gift to Beth, a sign of their love, had become Will and Beth's gift to Ivy.

Beth turned Ivy gently by the shoulders. "There. Looks

good." Beth smiled into Ivy's eyes. For a moment Ivy felt the peace that comes only in the presence of a friend who can read your heart.

"I'm headed to bed," Beth said. "Tell Tristan that Will and I send our love."

Six

IVY DIDN'T CALL TRISTAN UNTIL SHE REACHED THE intersection of Cockle Shell Road and Nauset Heights. "Hey," she said, "did I wake you up?"

"No. I was just about to start Lacey's movie."

Ivy smiled. "Keep the volume down, or you might not hear me whistling for Billy Bigelow."

"You're coming?"

The joy in his voice went straight to her heart.

"Yes, by foot. I'll be there in thirty minutes."

A kayak trip, a half mile across Nauset Harbor rather

77

than the two miles by land, would have been much faster, but having used that mode twice before, Ivy didn't want to attract attention with another middle-of-the-night paddle. Carrying a backpack stuffed with supplies, she walked briskly, following a roundabout route through tree-lined streets to the other side of the harbor.

As she turned from Beach Road onto Brick Hill, she paused to shift the weight of her backpack. That's when she heard it: the soft sound of crushed leaves, a hasty step backward into the brush alongside the road.

Ivy's heart skipped a beat. Bryan? Or was it Chase possessed by Gregory, tracking Ivy and hoping to find her "new" love?

Fighting the urge to turn around, she walked on steadily as if she'd heard nothing, but her mind raced to figure out who was following her and why.

A car's headlights brightened the roadway, and Ivy stepped quickly into a cluster of shrubs. She waited until she could no longer hear the engine, before emerging from the bushes. Amid the chirp of crickets, she heard stones crunching underfoot as her pursuer stepped onto the edge of the asphalt.

When Ivy had left the cottage, she had taken the route through the woods between Aunt Cindy's place and the main road. So whoever was stalking her had already had his chance to grab her. And he had another perfect opportunity now, she realized, on the dark stretch of road as she passed Ice House Pond. But he wasn't taking it. He wasn't going to hurt her, she reasoned, because he first wanted to see where she was going.

She approached a familiar triangle. The road bending to the right led to Tristan; Ivy took the fork to the left.

Checking the position of the egg-shaped moon, she tried to remember the layout of the roads. On a map Nauset Harbor looked more like a river than a harbor, bending back on itself as it meandered inland, becoming Town Cove, with homes along the shore and a series of public landings. She headed in that direction.

She longed to face down her pursuer. The tension of continuing on calmly wore on her nerves and turned her fear into anger. She kept reminding herself that Tristan's safety was what mattered. Rather than confront, she had to deceive the person looking for him.

She was near the cove now, and she started searching for just the right house, one with window shades closed and no car or lights, a place where a fugitive might be hiding. She began to think it was impossible, then she saw it—*perfect*—with its grass too long and a piece of advertising stuck in the frame of the door. Ivy circled the house and deposited her pack of supplies on the back step. After three sharp raps on the door, she hurried on, hoping to gain enough separation to turn around and observe her stalker.

She was about a hundred yards down the road when an alarm went off. Ivy turned back and saw the blinking floodlights. The house where she'd left the backpack had been wired! Her pursuer had probably forced a window. The lights in neighboring houses came on. Ivy laughed to herself and took off for home.

She ran all the way, figuring that her stalker had rushed off to his own safe harbor. She knew Tristan would be worried. As soon as she reached the inn's parking lot, she rested against her car and pulled out her phone.

A branch snapped underfoot. She spun around.

"Hello, Ivy," Chase said, emerging from the trees. He was out of breath. She guessed that he had taken the route through the woods, while she had kept to the main roads.

"Chase." She studied him, looking for some sign that Gregory was possessing him. "What are you doing here?"

"Following you."

"Really?" she replied with false cheerfulness. "Then you're back to where you started." Sliding her phone in her pocket, she felt for her keys. The car key had an alarm button.

"Ivy, if you keep running supplies to Luke, sooner or later the police are going to catch up with you."

"Especially if you tell them," she said.

"I can help you, Ivy."

"No thanks."

She started to move past him, but he reached out and pulled her back by the belt loop. It was one of Gregory's habits. Ivy's skin crept.

"It would be safer for you if we worked together," he said.

His eyes were normal, but his voice . . . That was it, she realized. The darkness was in his voice. Still, she continued to speak to him as if he was simply Chase. "Luke is an accused murderer. I wouldn't recommend that you help him."

"I would enjoy it," he replied. "I'm a great admirer of murderers, especially those who do it with passion. They're powerful. With their own hands, they squeeze out life, even that of the people they once loved." Chase slowly flexed his fingers, studying them, then smiled at Ivy. "Admit it, Ivy. You like bad boys." He moved his face close to hers.

Ivy turned away, revulsion thick in her throat.

His laughter was harsh. "All right," he said. "We can pretend, if you want to, that I don't know what's inside you, and that you haven't guessed what's inside me. But never forget: I know you, Ivy, your secret dreams, your secret fears—I know the most hidden part of your soul."

Ivy crossed her arms in front of her, feeling exposed, her spirit as well as her body. "Just leave Luke out of this," she said. "This is between you and me, Gregory."

His fake smile disappeared. For a moment the eyes that

Ivy gazed into were as empty as the sockets in a graveyard skull. She felt as if she was peering into hell.

"Till we meet again," Gregory said, then turned and left.

"IN CHASE!" TRISTAN REPEATED INTO THE PHONE. "IVY, are you okay?" He had been pacing for the last half hour, knowing that something was wrong. It wasn't like Ivy to be late and not call. "Where are you—I'll meet you."

"No, really, I'm fine. I'm just outside the cottage. Can you survive on the supplies you have?"

Tristan glanced at the pile of candy wrappers on the table next to the recliner. "Sure. One of the kids left a stash of Snickers and chocolate chip granola bars in the back of his closet."

"They didn't leave anything better in the kitchen cupboards?"

"You mean anything better than chocolate and nuts?" Tristan sighed loudly into the phone. "I guess I could look."

He heard Ivy laugh. Tristan's heart had finally stopped pounding with fear. Sitting on the couch, he stared at a muted video of Lacey racing through a house of bizarre-looking squirrels.

"Gregory doesn't seem to have any idea that you're in Luke's body," Ivy said to Tristan. "He was telling me about his admiration for murderers. Maybe he thinks I've finally developed good taste in guys."

Tristan laughed roughly.

"But you know how he works," Ivy went on. "He goes after anyone who's close to me. You're probably number one on his list. Or maybe, since he thinks you're a killer, he's looking for an ally. Anyway, it's just a matter of time till he finds you."

"I look forward to it," Tristan replied. "I'm tempted to take a long walk on the beach west of the church. That's where you said his house was, right?"

"Tristan, no! Don't even joke about it."

Tristan crumpled a candy wrapper into a tight little ball. Hour after hour, day after day, waiting, unable to do anything—

"Tristan?"

"I heard you."

He had spoken too sharply; her sudden silence told him that.

Tristan got up, climbed the short flight of steps to the kitchen, and started opening cupboard doors, scanning their contents with a flashlight. "Lots of healthy stuff here," he said into the phone. "Tuna fish, pasta, cans of soup. So don't worry."

"Good." She sounded relieved. "Listen, Mom, Andrew, and Philip are coming to the inn tomorrow, just overnight before they head up to Boston. It's going to make things a little complicated."

"I understand. I want you to stay safe and hang out with Philip."

"I love you, Tristan." Her voice quavered.

"I love you, Ivy. Always."

After hanging up, Tristan opened a can of tuna, ate a forkful, then put it in the fridge. Carrying his flashlight into the living room, he shone it on a quaintly illustrated map that hung above a chest. Tracing its roads with the narrow beam of his light, he located the old church, the public beach where Mike Steadman had been struck dead, and the private beach west of it, where Gregory now resided.

It was close enough to walk.

Seven

"DRAW THAT," PHILIP INSTRUCTED WILL. "IVY WEAR-
ing sea tinsel."

Beth glanced up and smiled. "I like that description."

Ivy fingered the pile of dark, papery sea grass that
Philip had artfully arranged on her head. "I assume I'm the
bad guy in this story."

"Yup," Will said, his pencil moving swiftly. "But I'll
change the nose, and no one will recognize you."

Beth laughed. Her own pencil had been moving fast
since they'd spread their towels on the beach. From where

Ivy sat, it looked like poems rather than stories, but Beth framed her notebook with her body, making it hard for someone else to read.

Ivy's mother, stepfather, and Philip had arrived at noon, and Ivy had joined them after work. They had set up camp behind the dunes, on the long spit of land that was the end of Nauset Beach, facing Nauset Harbor rather than the ocean. It was low tide, with the mud flats exposed, their wet surface shimmering with blue sky and clouds, reflecting the perfect summer day. Aunt Cindy had armed Philip with sand rakes and a wire basket for clamming, with the promise to show him how to make "chowda."

"Ready, champ?" Andrew asked, picking up the rakes.

Ivy's mother and stepfather had just returned from a walk—holding hands—which made Ivy smile. Beth gazed at them for a moment, then scribbled madly, perhaps something about love after forty.

"Don't forget the basket, Philip," Andrew said.

Ivy watched her stepfather and brother stroll side by side toward the flats. "Philip walks like Andrew."

Her mother, after much arranging, settled into her sand chair. "I know."

"How does that happen? They don't have the same body structure."

Her mother smiled. "It's love, not birth, that makes a child."

An hour later, Ivy tried her hand at clamming, and Philip was eager to teach her how. She heard in his instructions an echo of Andrew.

"Go easy. Feel the ridge? Spread your fingers like this. That's the way."

Ivy smiled at the little-boy version of the soft huskiness of Andrew's voice.

"Dig with your fingers on each side. Ease it out," Philip told her.

Hands coated with black sand, Ivy held up her trophy.

Philip raised a triumphant fist, something Andrew didn't do.

When the basket was full of clams, Andrew and her mother carried it back to the inn. Ivy and Philip paddled about in the tandem kayak. Philip, rowing in the front, sang like a drunken pirate, then scrunched down and laid his head back, staring straight up at the sky. "It's so deep," he said.

Ivy glanced upward and smiled. She had always thought of the sky as high, but she liked imagining it as deep, another ocean.

Philip dropped his arm over the side of the kayak. Sunlight, reflecting off the water, danced on his smooth cheek. "I wish I knew how far away heaven really is."

"Why?"

"So I'd know how long it takes for Tristan to go back and forth."

Ivy stopped paddling. "What?"

"So I can be home the next time he visits."

She caught her oar just before it slipped into the water. "What do you mean, 'the next time'?"

"I think—I'm pretty sure—he came to our house while we were away."

"Because?" Ivy asked.

"He missed me."

She laughed lightly, but her heart was beating fast. "He can't help but miss you, Philip. I meant, what makes you think he was at our house? Tristan went on to the Light, remember?"

"Well, that's what we *said*," her brother replied. "But it's likely we were wrong."

It's likely—another Andrewism.

"Mark Teixeira was moved," Philip went on. "On my baseball rug, the bases were loaded, and Mark Teixeira was up at bat."

Philip was talking about his baseball cards. Ivy had watched Tristan move the cards around the bases and had told him that Philip never forgot where he left his players.

"Someone made Mark hit a grand slam. Tristan would do that."

Ivy let the boat drift. Should she tell Philip the truth?

For herself, knowing that Tristan was here with them out-weighed all the risks created by that knowledge. But what was better for her brother?

"Couldn't Lacey have done it?"

"No, she thinks baseball's boring. I wish that Tristan had waited till I got back." Philip sighed. "Sometimes I talk to him, even though he doesn't answer. I still miss him. A lot. Do you?"

Ivy's throat felt tight, keeping her from answering right away.

Philip sat straight up and turned to look at her. "You don't?"

"Every day I'm not with him, I miss him," Ivy said.

"Why did God take him away?"

"God didn't," she replied firmly. "Gregory did."

"Then why did God let it happen?"

"I don't know, Philip."

"Neither does Dad."

They were three-quarters of the way across the harbor—so close, Tristan could have come out on the deck and waved to them. It would help Tristan to see Philip. And Philip had always been able to keep her secrets when they were living in the same house as Gregory.

"Did you tell Dad that you think Tristan came to our house?"

Philip shook his head. "Some things you can't say to other people. Dad would probably freak out if I told him Lacey likes to sit in his recliner. After she leaves, I always have to push it back in."

Ivy laughed out loud, but tears were in her eyes.

"Lacey said you're friends with that guy from the hospital."

"Luke," Ivy responded. "What else did Lacey say?"

"That he's hiding from the police, but he didn't really hurt anybody. Is she right?"

Ivy heard the trace of worry in her brother's voice. "Absolutely right. I'm trying to help him."

"Why?"

"Because I care about him."

Philip frowned. "More than you care about Will?"

"*Different* than the way I care about Will."

"Different than the way you care about *Tristan*?"

This kid didn't miss much. "More like the way I care about Tristan."

Philip looked over his shoulder at her, appraising her with a long, surprisingly adult gaze. All that he had been through had made him wiser than his years, Ivy thought. Her heart rather than her head made the decision: She paddled toward the opposite shoreline.

"Where we going?" Philip asked.

"To see a friend."

"Luke?"

"That's right." She'd leave it to Tristan to tell Philip who he was.

Philip was silent while they towed the kayak onto the narrow strip of sandy shore and walked a roundabout route to the house. When they were ten feet from the front door, hidden from the street by a cluster of bushes, Ivy whistled a melody from *Carousel*. Philip listened as she whistled the song twice, his eyes wide with curiosity. A brass latch turned, operated from the inside, and the main door fell inward about an inch.

Ivy glanced toward the street, then whispered to Philip, "Walk like we come here all the time."

She entered first and Tristan's arms encircled her.

"I've brought someone to see you, Luke," Ivy said, letting Tristan know she hadn't revealed his identity.

Tristan let go of her. His face lit up. "Philip!"

Philip looked him up and down, his lips pressed together—measuring "Luke" against two very high standards, the Tristan he had known and Will.

Tristan smiled at him. "Do you remember me? From the hospital."

"Yes." Philip's answer was clipped.

Tristan reached into his jeans pocket, then stretched out his hand. In his palm lay Philip's angel coin. "You gave me this. I'm never without it."

Philip's eyes dropped to the gold coin. "I thought you needed it."

"You were right."

Philip began to reach for it, then withdrew his hand.

After a long silence, Tristan asked uncertainly, "Do you want it back?"

"I want *Ivy* to have it."

Ivy saw the flicker of hurt pass over Tristan's face, though he covered it up quickly. She wanted to tell him that Philip saw him as an intruder taking Tristan's place in her heart. "Philip and I were just talking about Tristan," she said, "how much he misses him, how he still talks to him even though Tristan doesn't answer."

Tristan nodded, then handed Ivy the coin.

"Let's sit down," she said. "You still have that great movie in the VCR?"

"Oh, yeah," Tristan replied, his eyes still on Philip, "and I discovered four others. Got a whole Lacey Lovett film fest."

"You have Lacey's movies?" Philip asked.

"Right this way," he said, leading them back to the family room. "You have a favorite?"

"I've only seen one," Philip replied. "A friend pinched it for me."

Pinched. Philip was a word sponge, Ivy decided. He'd probably picked up that expression from his friend Lacey and didn't know it meant stealing.

They sat on the sofa in front of the big-screen TV, Philip sticking close to Ivy, Tristan sitting down on the other side of her. He reached for a stack of DVDs and handed them to Philip, who sorted through them, reading the descriptions on the backs.

Tristan couldn't take his eyes off Philip, and Ivy realized he had missed her brother as much as her brother had missed him. When Tristan finally glanced at Ivy, she read the question in his haunted eyes. *Tell him?*

"It's up to you," she whispered.

Tristan swallowed hard and looked away. Ivy wondered if he was afraid of Philip's reaction. Tristan knew he was Philip's hero. Did he imagine that Philip would love him less because he no longer had angel powers?

"Where's *The Revenge of the Zombie Soccer Mom*?" Philip asked, opening the empty plastic case.

"In the player. Want to watch some of it? Lacey Lovett is the soccer mom's daughter—and growing up just like her."

"Sounds good," Philip said enthusiastically, then, as if catching himself at being friendly, added coolly, "I guess so. Doesn't matter to me."

At the hospital, before Tristan remembered who he was, Philip had been instinctively drawn to him. Ivy was hoping that Philip would now perceive some sign of Tristan inside Luke; it would reassure Tristan that the same soul was still shining within him. But that wasn't going to happen, she thought, not as long as Philip saw this stranger as competi-tion for the Tristan he had loved so.

"It was just getting interesting," Tristan told Philip, clicking on the remote.

While the frames of horror, so bizarre they were comi-cal, flitted across the screen, Ivy saw a different set of scenes: Philip and Tristan on the floor of her music room, playing checkers; Tristan wearing a party hat as Philip's guest of honor at his family birthday dinner; Tristan and Philip in tuxes, the first time they met.

At the wedding reception for Andrew and her mother, both of them had slipped away to the kitchen storeroom. Tristan, having showered the bridal party with a tray of fresh vegetables, had been fired from his job as server, and was waiting for his friend, who was still working. Philip, upset, afraid, wanting no part of his new life with Andrew and Gregory, had found the same hiding place. When Ivy pulled open the storeroom door in search of Philip, there was the big sports hero from school, the famous Tristan Carruthers, entertaining her brother—unbelievably—by wearing salad greens on his head and olives on his teeth, a stalk of celery protruding from each ear, a shrimp tail stuck in his nostril.

Ivy laughed to herself.

"What the heck?" Tristan exclaimed, pointing to the big screen and the strange thing emerging from a movie sewer to stalk zombie Lacey. "What's that supposed to be?"

Philip, forgetting his coolness, chortled. "He's not very scary."

"Looks like someone fertilized him," Tristan said.

Philip nodded. "Looks like dead celery's growing out of his ears."

"Got a salad on his head."

"Shrimp sticking out of his nose," Philip added.

"Gross," said Ivy.

"Some black olives—" Tristan began.

"On his teeth," Philip interjected quickly.

Ivy felt her brother shifting in his seat next to her, leaning forward, looking across her to Tristan. Tristan turned his head slightly to the right. The profile was Luke's, but the memory, the boyish humor, was someone else's.

Philip got up and stood in front of Tristan. Bending forward, he peered into Tristan's eyes as if he was trying to see beneath the surface of a pond.

Tristan gazed back at him steadily. At last he spoke. "I've been wondering what inning it was when Mark Teixeira hit the grand slam."

"Tristan!" Philip said softly, breathing the name like a prayer.

Tristan nodded.

"Tristan!" Philip's face was alight with wonder.

"Hey, buddy." Tristan's voice shook. "I've missed you. Still beating people at checkers?"

Philip broke into a grin. "Not anymore. I'm learning chess."

"Chess! No! Now I'll never win!" Tristan exclaimed. "Unless, of course, Lacey helps me cheat."

Ivy's brother laughed as if this was the funniest joke in the world. Tristan laughed with him, then laughed harder when Philip forced his own chuckle to sound deep.

Tristan put his arms around Philip. Philip hugged him tightly and squeezed his eyes shut, but Ivy saw the tear escape down her little brother's cheek.

TRISTAN HADN'T REALIZED HOW RAW HE'D FEEL when seeing Philip again. Philip talked about a million miles per hour—summer camp, California, his year in school since Tristan had left. Finally, the question Tristan had expected and dreaded was asked: "How come you came back as another person?"

"We're not sure," Ivy said quickly, covering for him.

"I fell," Tristan replied, then told Philip exactly what had happened.

Afterward Philip sat quietly for a very long minute, as if thinking things through. "It was because you love Ivy. Me too."

"You too? No kidding!" Tristan quipped.

"I would have kissed her and brought her back to life."

Tristan almost cried: Philip's understanding felt like forgiveness.

He saw Ivy quickly wipe the corner of her eye, then she rose to her feet. "Philip, we have to go. Remember, if anybody asks, we were just exploring. No one can know Tristan—*or Luke*—is here."

Philip nodded. He gave Tristan a solemn hug good-bye and followed Ivy to the vestibule. At the door he turned and looked up at Tristan searchingly. "You came back after a long time," the little boy said. "Can Gregory?"

Ivy and Tristan exchanged glances. Philip saw them and answered his own question: "He can."

"If you think you see Gregory, do you know what to do?" Tristan asked.

"Run."

"Good. And call out to Lacey," Tristan said. "After that, if you can do it safely, call Ivy, and she'll call me. Beth and Will are also on the lookout. You'll be okay, buddy."

"And Ivy will be okay?"

"Hey," Ivy said lightly, "it's all of us and just one of him."

But Philip wasn't so easily convinced. He looked to Tristan for confirmation that their numbers would be enough.

Tristan couldn't lie to him. "I'll do my best to keep her safe, I promise."

After they left, Tristan felt on edge and paced like a caged animal, moving from room to room. He tried to distract himself, playing another round of his detective game, piecing together the story of the family who spent their summers there. Nicholas and Sarah—he had found their names on framed certificates for sailing and gymnastics—were close to Philip's age. Michael, the victim of Gregory's lightning strike, had shared a room with Nicholas. What had it been like for those kids to lose their big brother? Tristan had felt Philip's tears against his arm and for a moment thought his own heart would break. If Philip lost Ivy—

It didn't have to be this way, Tristan thought. Right now he had the advantage, knowing who and where Gregory was. When Gregory possessed Beth, his growth in power was gradual, but the night she tried to kill Ivy, Beth's grasp had far exceeded her natural strength. Tristan needed to find out what kind of powers Chase had now, and take him on before Gregory's strength grew. He had to protect Ivy— he had promised Philip.

Checking the map in the living room and estimating the walk would take close to two hours—too long to chance being recognized—Tristan decided to borrow some clothes. From Mr. Steadman's closet he chose slacks and a preppy-looking shirt with long sleeves that could be rolled up: the guise of a lawyer on vacation. He debated whether to add a pristine-looking baseball cap. Where was Lacey when you needed wardrobe advice? But ever since the night she, Ivy, and he had hashed things out—and he'd rejected her theories—she had been giving him the cold shoulder.

Tristan's hair was still dyed a dark color, but he was clean-shaven now, not like the police artist's rendering of Luke with a scruffy beard. Bareheaded was better for his new image, he thought. On his way back from the closet, wearing a pair of boat shoes that were just a little snug, he passed Mrs. Steadman's bureau. The beam of his flashlight caught on something shiny: Gold hoop earrings. Tristan grinned and snatched one, slipping it on the ring finger of his left hand. Twentysomething, successful, married, he thought, hoping he could fake it if he met a few dog walkers or a touring police car.

As soon as it was dark, he headed out. Almost two hours later, Tristan stood at the edge of a cobblestone drive, studying a house that matched Ivy's description of Chase's. The name on the mailbox, Holloway, confirmed that Tristan was in the right place.

There were lights on upstairs and down, and the second-floor windows were open. A dog's deep *woof* was answered by a woman's voice: "Hush, Plato."

Tristan crept to the garage, a large building with three bays. Quietly opening the side door, he stepped inside and clicked on his flashlight. The only vehicle was a Mercedes sedan, not the kind of car Chase was likely to drive. The garage was neatly maintained, with garden tools, clamming rakes, bikes, and windsurfers hanging from the walls and ceiling, leaving space for two other cars.

The sound of an engine caught Tristan's attention. Suddenly, there was a click above him. The garage light went on, and one of the three automatic doors began to rise. Tristan quickly extinguished his flashlight and stepped back into the frame of the side door. As soon as the car's headlights entered the garage, he exited and hid in the shadow of the building.

Chase emerged and stood looking at his house across the stone driveway. Was he seeing it as Gregory would see it? Tristan wondered. How much control over Chase did Gregory have at the moment?

Something stirred by a lamppost at the end of the house path, and after a moment Tristan realized a cat was moving toward them. The gray-striped tabby trotted in Chase's direction, then stopped, stretching its head forward, sniffing, as if uncertain. Tristan suspected that it belonged to the Holloways.

Chase hissed at it.

The cat remained where it was, though its eyes were wary now.

Chase, standing by the garage's downspout, glanced around, then leaned over and picked up a fist-size rock. He called the tabby, which walked slowly toward him. Images of Ivy's cat, the one Gregory had killed, flashed through Tristan's mind. When Chase raised his arm to hurl the rock, Tristan couldn't hold back. He charged him.

"What the—" Chase swore aloud.

They grappled and rolled on the cobblestones. Lights came on—floodlights, Tristan realized. Chase scrambled to his feet, but Tristan didn't let go. He dragged Chase through the open bay of the garage.

"Chase?" It was the voice of the woman who had shushed the dog. "Is that you?"

Tristan had him in a stranglehold. "Answer her," he commanded. "Tell her you'll be there in a few minutes."

"Just me," Chase called back. "I'll be in soon."

"Tigger is still out," the woman replied. "See if you can find him. G'night."

Tristan relaxed his grip and Chase wriggled free. "I ought to hang that cat," he said, then looked Tristan up and down in the dim light that came through the open garage bay. "Well, look at you," he mocked. "I didn't know they wore Tommy Hilfiger in River Gardens."

So Chase had guessed that he was "Luke."

"You know," Chase said, "you're barely recognizable in the police photos, the enhanced ones they distributed to the media. If I were you, I'd be insulted."

Tristan responded with a sardonic smile.

"I checked the old photos, of course." Chase picked up

a folding chair, snapped it open, then set a second one next to it and gestured for Tristan to sit down. "I've been looking for you."

"So I heard," Tristan replied. "What do you want?"

"To help you."

At that, Tristan laughed.

"Don't be so cynical. I believe in justice—you, getting what you deserve. Others, getting what they had coming. What did she do to you, your old girlfriend Colleen?"

"Corinne," Tristan corrected, moving his chair a foot away from Chase before sitting down.

"She definitely got under your skin."

Tristan nodded and continued to play the role of Luke. "She cheated on me. She cheated and lied to my face."

"Left you pissing mad. Left you with no choice."

Tristan lifted his flashlight beam as far as Chase's neck. His tendons looked like tightened cords. He was being eaten up by anger—Gregory's anger.

Chase pushed the light away. "Girls betray," he said. "It's in the genes."

"No kidding!"

"And then there was Alison. You've had some bad luck."

"Alicia," Tristan corrected.

According to Ivy, Chase prided himself on knowing more than anyone else; he would have gotten these details right. But Gregory wouldn't care—wouldn't bother to learn the names of people he thought irrelevant to his own happiness. Gregory was in control.

"What'd Alicia do to you?" he asked.

Tristan shrugged off the question. "More of the same. It's over now."

"It's never over."

Not when you hunger for revenge, Tristan thought.

Chase leaned forward. "They both deserved to die. You know that as well as I."

Tristan gritted his teeth, struggling to stay in his role as Luke. "Unfortunately, others don't see it that way."

"Screw them!" Chase dismissed the others with a flick of his hand. "Screw them all!" He moved his face close to Tristan's. "You made out okay. The dead girls, they're nothing compared to Ivy."

Tristan stood up.

"A jock like you," Chase continued, "you know *hot* when you see it. The other girls, they were okay . . . for lower class. But sexy little *Ivy*—"

"I'm not stupid!" Tristan said. He hated hearing the soft, insinuating voice talking about Ivy. It was like a snake's tongue wrapping around her name.

"Of course you're not." His tone was patronizing. "All the same, I've got some advice for you, Luke—one guy to another: Grab hold of that gold hair, give it a good yank, and don't let go. Teach her who's boss."

For a moment Tristan saw Ivy's glorious yellow tangle in his hands. The next instant he felt pressure inside his skull. Chase's body went rigid, as if Gregory was focusing all his power on breaking into Tristan's mind. A hot orange burning behind Tristan's eyes made his blood feel like fire. He staggered and dropped his flashlight, then sank to his knees. The pressure inside his head grew until he thought his mind would explode.

He pushed back. The pain was excruciating, his strength pitched against Gregory's, with Luke's skull a flimsy wall between them. Tristan shut his eyes and bore down with his spirit, praying for strength. *Angels—*

Suddenly, Gregory's force gave way. Tristan sat back hard on the concrete floor. He saw wires of light leave his splayed fingers and climb the walls, burning like long-tailed fuses. An overhead lamp exploded, then plunged them into darkness again. Tiny pieces of shattered plastic and glass rained down. Inside the Holloway house, the dog started barking.

Too weak to stand, Tristan crawled across the greasy floor to his flashlight. Hanging on to a door of the Mercedes, he pulled himself up and saw Chase slumped in his chair.

Chase raised his head slowly, staring at Tristan. "Who are you?" he asked. "*What* are you?"

Tristan leaned against the car, one hand rubbing his aching temple. "I thought you would have guessed by now."

Chase frowned, then cocked his head. "Do you hear that?"

"The dog?"

But a more ominous sound, murmuring voices, flowed over the deep throb in Tristan's brain. So Gregory heard the voices too!

"They're chanting *Tristan*."

The voices grew louder.

"God damn you! Tristan!"

"Hello, Gregory."

Gregory didn't attempt to hide his amazement. "You used to slip inside minds, but this is something different." He stood up and circled Tristan. "When I tried to break in, I felt just one mind, one soul—and it wasn't Luke McKenna's. He would've been an easy mark for me. Tell me how you did it."

Tristan remained silent.

"The voices taught you," Gregory guessed, his voice husky with desire. "The voices taught you something they haven't taught me! Tell me how"—a smile spread slowly over his face—"and I'll spare Ivy."

"You've always been a liar, Gregory."

"Not now. Now we're on the same side, Tristan. The dead side." His laughter ended in an electric hiss.

Beyond the garage, the driveway grew brighter; the floodlights had been switched on again.

"Chase?" the woman called. "Is everything okay?"

He grimaced, then punched a button on the wall, lowering the garage door. Tristan followed Gregory out the side entrance but remained in the shadows.

"Get out of our lives, Gregory," he said. "Go back to where you belong."

Gregory laughed at him. "Don't you know? I bring hell with me wherever I go." Then he sauntered across the lawn. "Coming, Mother."

Eight

"HEY, BRYAN, YOU MADE IT!" MAX CALLED OUT, Monday afternoon.

Ivy, who had been following Max down the long dock where the Moyers kept their boats, stopped in her tracks. Bryan was stretched out, sunning himself on the bench of a powerboat tied up near the end of the walkway.

"Bryan!" Kelsey exclaimed, sounding as pleasantly surprised as Max.

"Hey, babe. You know I wouldn't miss a chance to be on the water with you. And Ivy." He sat up, spreading his arms over the back of the padded bench. "Where's Beth and Will?"

Good old Mr. Congeniality, Ivy thought. "Stand-up paddling," she answered aloud, and resumed her inventory of the Moyers' fleet.

She figured that Bryan wouldn't have used anything with a sail the night he murdered Luke. And the cigarette boat, like an expensive sports car, would have attracted too much attention. The cabin cruiser, with its fishing lines, would have been clumsy and hard to wash down. But the boat that Max had described as a twenty-four-foot bow rider, the one Bryan was lounging on now, would have been perfect for the job.

Bryan took an ice chest from Max, then offered a hand to Kelsey, who leaped lightly into the boat. Reaching next for Ivy's hand, he held it too long and squeezed her fingers hard enough to hurt. She got his message: He was in control—at least, he wanted to be.

"Hey, Maxie, can I drive?" Bryan asked. "I know where Ivy wants to go. Lighthouse Beach."

"No, there's been a change in plans," Ivy told him breezily. "Kelsey wants to hang out at South Beach."

"Well, it's probably safer," Bryan observed. "The currents at Lighthouse Beach are pretty wicked. Did you know people drown there?"

"Really?" Ivy replied.

He laughed.

"You know that, Ivy," Kelsey said. "That's where Luke almost died."

"*Almost,*" Bryan echoed.

Ivy hated these verbal games. She turned away, watching Max open and close compartments as he prepared to cast off. There were a lot of places to hide things, and all Bryan would have needed was a place to stow a syringe and a fresh change of clothes, in case his own got bloody. In one of the boat compartments, a pair of knives and a heavy wrench glinted among other useful tools. There was plenty of rope for tying someone up. The long pole on the floor would be handy for pushing a body away from the boat. Cleanup would be easy, and expected after an ocean outing, the dock hoses right there. In fact, Ivy began to wonder why all premeditated murders didn't occur on boats.

"Planning to get yourself one?" Bryan asked Ivy, and shot her a false smile.

She turned her attention back to Max's preparations. He was checking the weather radar. "How's it look, Captain?"

"Good for now," Max replied. "But we'll have to keep an eye out for squalls." He glanced over his shoulder. "Finally! Here comes Dhanya."

Bryan turned around. "And Chase. You invited *him*?"

"I invited Dhanya," Max replied with a shrug.

Kelsey grimaced. "I hope Chase is feeling better. If he gets seasick, I'm throwing him over."

"Allow me," Bryan said, with a sly look at Ivy. "I'm good at it."

Ivy ignored the remark. Although she feared Bryan, as long as she didn't let him separate her from the crowd, she'd be safe on this trip. The greater danger now, the threat to all of them, was the guy following Dhanya down the planks.

How much control did Gregory have over Chase? If Gregory demanded from his host something insane or violent, would Chase have the inner strength to refuse?

Chase was quiet as he stepped onboard, his face expressionless, his mouth almost slack beneath contoured sunglasses that hugged his cheekbones. When Ivy asked him how he was feeling, he answered with just one word, "fine," then turned away.

Dhanya and he chose two of the luxurious leather seats behind the cockpit. Bryan took Kelsey's hand and pulled her toward the front of the speedboat. The windshield and console could be opened in the center, and the V-shaped area in front of the cockpit had padded leather benches where guests could enjoy plenty of sea spray when the boat was moving. For the next fifteen minutes, with Max standing at the helm and Ivy in the seat across from him, they roared through the channel. Then Max cut the engine and eased his craft into the shallow water near the end of South Beach, where they moored with five other boats.

While Max dropped anchor, a water taxi puttered in and left off a handful of visitors. Three families beached on the west side by their boats. Others spread their blankets close to the ocean on the east side, which was a short walk via a path through the dunes. With Bryan carrying the ice chest on his shoulder, the six of them hiked to the ocean side.

Kelsey dropped her towel and bag and ran for the water. Bryan was just a few steps behind. Ivy, Dhanya, and Max set up camp, spreading blankets and anchoring them with their boat shoes. Chase stood apart from them all, surveying the area. Finally settling on the beach blanket next to Dhanya, he lay back without saying a word. Ivy saw Dhanya look at him uncertainly, then take out a book to read.

"Want to go for a walk?" Max asked Ivy. "The tide's low. Good time to look for shells."

Ivy was reluctant to leave Dhanya with Chase. She was also watching the horseplay between Kelsey and Bryan in the surf. Every time Kelsey stayed underwater for more than five seconds, Ivy held her breath.

"I don't feel like walking far," she said.

"I'm always happy to be lazy," Max replied.

He was always happy to do what anybody wanted.

"Can I tag along?" Dhanya asked. "Do you mind, Chase?"

Chase's response was to silently remove his T-shirt and sunglasses and lie back again on his towel. He draped the shirt over his face, shielding it from the sun—and them. Ivy studied him. Was this just Chase acting passive-aggressive? Or was Chase being muzzled while Gregory gathered his strength?

For the next half hour Ivy, Dhanya, and Max scoured the ocean's edge. Max reminded Ivy of Philip—maybe it was a guy thing—turning over dead horseshoe crabs and picking up anything slimy. Dhanya collected shiny stones, and Ivy a pile of shells. She told Max about the clam chowder they had made.

Max grinned. "When I was little, I told my dad I wanted to be a clammer."

Dhanya glanced up and giggled. "What did he say?"

"Great. But first I had to learn about retail clothing."

"If you could do anything you wanted, Max," Ivy said, "and live anywhere you liked, what would you choose?"

He didn't have to think long. "I'd live in New Orleans and go to jazz clubs every night."

Ivy looked at him, surprised. "Great! I'd come visit you." They talked for a long time about jazz, and Dhanya demonstrated the challenge of dancing to a syncopated rhythm. When she tried to teach Max a series of jazz steps, Ivy watched and applauded. For a while she was able to distance herself from the danger hovering nearby, then she glanced over her shoulder.

She had seen Kelsey and Bryan come out of the water, but they were gone now from the beach. Ivy stood up quickly.

"Everything okay?" Max asked.

"I think so. Did anyone see where Kelsey went?"

"Wherever Bryan went," Dhanya answered innocently.

Ivy started toward their blankets, her eyes sweeping the beach and water. Dhanya and Max followed.

"Chase, do you know where Kelsey and Bryan are?" Ivy asked.

He didn't respond.

Dhanya knelt next to him. "Chase?" She reached as if she was going to nudge him awake.

Ivy caught Dhanya's hand in midair. "I—I'd let him be," Ivy said, worried about how Gregory would react if caught off guard.

Dhanya studied him for a moment. "You're probably right. He's been a little . . . irritable."

Ivy, Dhanya, and Max played cards, with Ivy the first one out of every game, her concentration lost to watchfulness as she kept one eye out for Bryan and Kelsey and the other on Chase. After the third game, Max glanced at the sky, then walked back to the path between the dunes. He returned quickly.

"There's weather coming in from the west," he told them. "We should get back."

"What about Kelsey and Bryan?" Ivy asked.

Max stared up the beach, hands on his hips, frowning. The people thirty yards away from them were calling to their children and collecting their pails and shovels.

"Chase?" Dhanya said. "Come on, sleepyhead." When he didn't respond, she laid her hand on his arm.

Chase pulled away from her and turned over on his stomach, his face still hidden.

Max was losing patience. "We have to get moving. I don't want to be boating through a storm. Chase, wake up!" Max reached down and pulled the shirt off Chase's head.

Chase's eyes flew open and he sat up. His face was calm and his motion deliberate, but when Ivy looked into his gray eyes, she felt as if she was seeing the gathering storm.

"Do you know where Kelsey and Bryan are?" Max asked Chase.

"They came in from the water," Chase said, his voice a dark monotone, "picked up some beers, then went that direction." He pointed north.

"Max, why don't you get the coolers and stuff to the boat," Ivy suggested. "I'll run up the beach."

"Let Chase—" Max began.

"I'm faster."

With the strange, slow way Chase was reacting—only

his eyes moving, searching the sky in the west—Ivy didn't have to convince Max further.

"Stay with Max," Ivy said to Dhanya. "Do whatever *Max* says." Ivy took off.

After the first three minutes of running, she wished she had a watch with her. Distances were deceiving at the beach when there were no landmarks, just mile after mile of sand. Running in sand was exhausting, and she couldn't judge how far she'd gone by her body's tiredness. She turned back once and saw a family standing in pairs. She turned back a second time and there was no one, but whether those people had left or she had run beyond their visibility, she wasn't sure.

Bryan wouldn't hurt Kelsey, she told herself, pausing to catch her breath. He was too smart to shift the police's attention from Luke to him. As long as he kept his emotions under control, as long as he wasn't drunk and Kelsey didn't tease too hard . . . Ivy continued running.

She strained her eyes to see ahead. There was still blue sky to the east, but the sparkling Atlantic had dulled to a glimmer. Stopping again, she realized the ocean breeze had disappeared and the wind was coming in stronger over the dunes. Ivy had no desire to stand alone in the middle of a beach during a thunderstorm. She turned back, running, hoping that Bryan and Kelsey had crossed the dunes and walked back along the other side.

When she finally reached Max, she shook her head, then leaned over, hands on her knees, breathing hard. "How soon?" she asked. "How soon till we're safer staying here?"

The other boats had pulled up anchor. Ivy watched the distinctive red and white of the water taxi shrinking to a dot as it hurried its passengers back to the marina. The clouds in the west were like a gray ocean, each wave rolling higher, trying to lick as high as the sun. Chase stood at the edge of the water, gazing toward the storm, Dhanya halfway between him and Max.

"Here they come. Come on! Move it!" Max hollered to Kelsey and Bryan.

As Ivy had hoped, they were returning by the west side of the dunes. They took their time. She let Max run to them and prod while she waded to the boat with Chase and Dhanya.

The clouds had blotted out the sun, and the water suddenly felt colder. Ivy saw the goose bumps on Dhanya's wet arms as they splashed their way to the boat. As soon as Ivy boarded, she started opening compartments, looking for life vests.

She handed one to Dhanya, then Chase, who stood there, dangling it by his side. "Put it on," Ivy ordered as she slipped her own arms through one and fastened the clasp. Dhanya did, but Chase simply stood there looking over the side of the boat at the water slapping against it.

As soon as Kelsey climbed onboard, Ivy handed her a vest.

"I can swim."

"Doesn't matter."

Out of the corner of her eye, Ivy saw a vicious streak of lightning over North Monomoy.

Chase murmured something. Ivy handed Bryan a vest.

"Looking out for me?" he asked, sounding amused.

"As you know," Ivy snapped, "people who are knocked unconscious and fall overboard usually drown."

He laughed, and Ivy smelled the alcohol on his breath. She quickly turned to Max, who had slipped his arms through the vest she had tossed to him.

"Everyone sit down and hold on," he said.

Ivy fastened Max's vest for him while he started the engine. Kelsey and Bryan pushed past her to sit in the speedboat's open bow.

"No," Max barked at them. "Stay behind me for this ride."

"Oh, issit going to be exciting?" Kelsey asked, slurring her words.

"A little too exciting," he said, and flicked his head toward the stern of the boat.

But Kelsey and Bryan didn't move. Ivy felt the first drops of rain on her shoulders. Max's hand hovered over the throttle.

"Give me five seconds," she said to Max, and moved forward, picking up the life vest Kelsey had tossed onto the boat floor, then reaching for one of Kelsey's arms and forcing it through the hole. Kelsey laughed and lay back as limp as a rag doll. They didn't have time for games. Ivy yanked the vest around her back, then shoved her other arm through.

Bryan watched, grinning. "Me next?"

"No, you can handle it. Come on, Kelsey, let's sit with Dhanya."

"I sip wi' Dhanya al'time."

Ivy tried to pull her roommate to her feet, but she was dead weight.

Chase stood up, watching these events with interest, and moved forward to stand on the passenger side of the cockpit.

"I've got to start, Ivy," Max said, raising his voice above the wind and the marine radio. It crackled with squall warnings. "Come on back."

"In a sec." Ivy fastened Kelsey's life vest, then grabbed hold of the windshield, lurching through the cockpit divide as the boat moved forward in the rough water. Dropping down in the seat next to Dhanya, facing the stern, she watched the turgid green and gray wake spume out behind the boat.

Chase was talking to Max, but as the wind picked up, most of his words were blown away. "Go faster," Ivy heard

Chase shout. She turned around, hugging the seat, trying to see what was ahead.

"Faster!"

"Can't," Max shouted back. "We're already bucking."

Ivy saw a channel marker go by. The frenzied waves grew higher. The boat rode each peak coming at it, pitching its nose upward, then smacking down.

"Rid'em cowboy!" Bryan shouted.

"Yee-haw!" Kelsey started to stand up, then fell over on Bryan, laughing wildly.

"Stay down, Kelsey!" Ivy cried.

Lightning forked, ripping a seam in the sky.

"Please, Max, go faster," Dhanya begged.

"Have to hold a steady course."

"Not even fifty knots," Chase complained. "Let me drive."

"And flip us over?" Standing at the wheel, Max somehow kept his balance and forged ahead. Ivy wondered how he could see where he was going. *Angels, guide him,* she prayed.

Rain blew sideways. A wave broke over the side and washed backward to the stern.

Kelsey shrieked with laughter.

"Everybody okay?" Max shouted.

"We're fine," Ivy called back, trying to sound calm as thunder pounded and rolled over other volleys of thunder.

But more than the lightning and water, it was the darkness that scared her, the speed with which an ember of late afternoon could be plunged into a black vortex. It felt demonic.

Clinging to the back of her seat, she watched Chase. Had Gregory suddenly amassed that kind of power? But it didn't matter whether he had stirred up the storm. Once before, Gregory had created a single bolt of lightning. When the moment was right, he would strike again, killing them all.

How could she stop him? If she dove overboard, would he pursue her and leave the others alone? Ivy pushed up from her seat. But a half second too late she saw that she had guessed the wrong plan. Chase grabbed Max's arm with unnatural strength and turned the wheel. Stretching across Max, he shoved the throttle all the way down.

The boat jerked and climbed a wave at an impossible angle. It hung up there as if snagged on a jagged piece of lightning, then began to roll. Everything seemed to happen in slow motion: Kelsey screaming, Dhanya sliding past Ivy's hands, moments of being suspended in midair, shielded from the rain by the frame of the boat, then falling into the hungry sea.

The sea and its terrible darkness—Ivy couldn't see, couldn't move, couldn't fight her way to the surface. She felt the heavy water swirling around her and struggled to find her way up.

I'm under the boat—trapped beneath, she realized. She pushed off with her feet, then kicked and pulled with her arms, swimming sideways, not up, holding the last gasp of oxygen in her lungs until it was unbearable. *Angels!*

Lighter—it was lighter over there. She swam for the gray area. Surfacing, she opened her mouth to drink up air. Rain poured down her face.

"Who's there?" Ivy cried out. "Anyone?"

"Here!"

It was Dhanya, floating in her life vest, several feet away. White foam hissed down the sides of the waves between them. Ivy swam toward her.

"Dhanya? Ivy?" Max called out.

"Over here!"

"Keep together!" he shouted.

"Help me! Somebody help me! I can't hold him."

"Kelsey!" Ivy called back to her.

The sea's sickening heave continually shifted her horizon. Then she saw Kelsey struggling to hold on to Bryan, who was slumped in her arms, unconscious. Ivy swam to her. It took forever, the waves pushing her back. "Put one arm around me, so we can keep him between us," Ivy said.

"Where's Chase?" Max shouted.

"Chase!" Dhanya cried out. "Oh God, he's gone."

"Stay with Ivy," Max ordered her, then took off

swimming, stopping every few feet to call Chase's name. "Found him!" he yelled at last.

Ivy couldn't see either guy. With the rough seas, it was all the three girls could do to keep Bryan's head above water.

"Turn him on his back," Ivy said, "so his body will float."

They did, and Ivy gasped. There was a long, bloody gash on Bryan's temple. His green eyes were wide open, his mouth slack, his body limp. *He's dead,* she thought. A queer feeling passed over her—horror but relief. Bryan was dead.

Then his body convulsed and he started spitting up seawater.

"Hold tight!" Kelsey begged the others.

Bryan coughed in violent spasms. When his body finally grew quiet again, he closed his eyes. The second time he opened them, it was still raining, but the worst of the storm had passed. Max had towed Chase, semiconscious to where the others were floating and holding on to one another, half in shock.

Suddenly, Bryan pushed away from them. Treading water, he grinned, as if glorying in the strength of his arms and legs. He raised one fist above the sea. "Alive!" he shouted, then threw back his head and laughed up at the stormy heavens.

"Bryan, stay close," Max warned.

"Yes, Captain," Bryan replied cheerfully, and swam close to Ivy. Holding on to her life vest, he whispered in her ear, "Vengeance is mine."

Nine

AUNT CINDY STRODE TOWARD THEM. "MY HAIR'S going to be snow white by the end of this summer," she said, pushing back a swath of it that showed just a few silver strands. She looked from Ivy to Kelsey to Dhanya, who were sitting three abreast in the ER waiting room. Beth and Will had rushed in behind her.

"The Coast Guard briefed me," Aunt Cindy went on. "I *am* glad you all had the good sense to wear life vests."

Kelsey glanced sideways at Ivy; Ivy kept quiet.

"Next time, before boating, try checking the marine forecast!"

"But the squall came up really quick," Kelsey argued with her aunt. "We weren't the only ones caught by surprise."

"Like I said, I'll be snow white by next month."

"How's Chase doing?" Beth asked. "And Max and Bryan?"

Ivy filled them in. When Max rescued Chase, Chase was halfway out of his life vest and shifting in and out of consciousness. He was physically stable now, but confused, and undergoing tests. Bryan had received stitches and was being checked for a concussion. "They may be keeping both of them overnight." For a few hours, Ivy thought, she and her roommates would be safe.

Ivy had already been cross-examined by Chase's father, who was now talking to Max's dad and Bryan's uncle. Mr. Holloway had refused to believe that his son was at the helm when the boat flipped over. Aunt Cindy headed across the waiting room to talk to them.

When her aunt was out of earshot, Kelsey turned to Ivy. "Thanks for not telling."

Ivy nodded.

"About the life vest, I mean. And thanks for making me wear it."

Ivy nodded a second time. Every nerve in her body felt tightened and plucked, like the strings of an instrument.

"You mad at me?" Kelsey asked.

"Yes."

But Ivy was more than mad. She was frightened—for Kelsey, the others, and herself. Kelsey had been hanging all over Bryan on the way to the hospital—hanging all over a murderer possessed by a demon.

"I couldn't help it. I was drunk."

"You can help being drunk," Ivy replied, her voice shaking. She struggled to regain her composure. "Kelsey, when you drink you make yourself vulnerable. Anyone who wants to take advantage of you, can."

"Like Bryan?" Kelsey asked with a smile.

"Anyone!" Ivy snapped. "Why do you want to be out of control? Why do you want to let *someone else* control you? That's what happens, you know!"

Kelsey was silent for a moment. "It's fun . . . as long as I'm with somebody I trust."

Ivy knew that an argument against trusting "Bryan" would make him all the more appealing. "And if *that* person is drunk and out of control?" *And a demon*, she thought.

"Ivy, you're going to bore your college friends to death."

Ivy wanted to throttle her. She stood up abruptly and walked away, pushing through the automatic door to the hospital parking lot. Outside she took deep breaths of the evening air.

It hadn't rained in Hyannis; the storm was just an afternoon squall that had nicked the elbow of Cape Cod. Had Gregory caused the storm, or had he simply taken advantage of it? What did it matter, she told herself, the result was the same.

"Ivy," Will said, catching her arm lightly. He and Beth had followed her outside. "What really happened?"

She had to tell them, she thought. They needed to be on guard and to help her protect Kelsey.

"Was Gregory involved?" Beth asked.

Ivy took a deep breath. "He was in Chase."

"When the boat overturned," Will guessed.

"Yes. Bryan, the real Bryan, died in the accident."

Beth's hand went up to her mouth, muffling a scream.

"Gregory is in Bryan the same way Tristan is in Luke. Bryan's body is Gregory's now."

Will swore. "It's going to be Gregory and Suzanne all over again! Ivy, be careful. You remember how Gregory used Suzanne to get at you."

"We all have to be careful." That warning was enough, Ivy thought; she didn't need to endanger Beth and Will by revealing information about Bryan's crimes.

Will glanced at Beth. "I think you should tell Ivy about your vision."

"So that's coming back too!" Ivy said. Beth was truly herself again, with her psychic gift as well as her writing.

"When we were paddling today, I kept seeing an image in the water." With her finger Beth made a circle. "A snake swallowing its tail."

"What does it mean?" Ivy asked.

"You know how it is with these visions," Beth replied. "When interpreting them, all I have to go by is a feeling."

"Which is?"

"I think that things are coming full circle. Be aware, Ivy. Somehow, your battle with Gregory will come back to where it started."

WHEN IVY FINISHED WORK TUESDAY AFTERNOON and was returning to the cottage with Kelsey, she found Dusty on the front step, his eyes dilated, his tail whipping back and forth.

"What's gotten into him?" Kelsey asked.

"I don't know," Ivy said, then a chill ran up her spine. Nudging Dusty out of the way, she yanked open the screen door.

Bryan lay stretched out on the girls' sofa. "Hey," he said, and lifted the soda he'd helped himself to. "Can I fix you girls something to drink?"

Max, who was sitting on the chair near the sofa, must

have read the unwelcoming expression on Ivy's face. "I told him we should wait outside."

Ivy felt invaded, but Kelsey hurried past her and threw her arms around Bryan. He sat up laughing.

"You look a mess!" Kelsey said.

A bandage covered the gash on his temple. With all the blood last night, Ivy hadn't noticed the bruising, which covered his cheekbone down to his jaw.

Bryan met Ivy's stare. "It's nice to see you again."

"How are you feeling, Ivy?" Max asked.

"Okay," she answered shortly. "You?"

"Not much in the mood for boating," he replied with a wry smile.

He looked tired, and his eternal tan had turned a funny shade of brown, as if he had gone pale beneath it.

"Max has been playing nurse," Bryan said. "I don't know what I'd do without him."

Kelsey sat down on the sofa with Bryan. "I can take over for a while."

"It's a concussion," Max informed them. "Uncle Pat sure wasn't happy. Bryan can't be on the ice till his symptoms disappear—can't risk falling and doing more damage."

"So I'm on vacation," Bryan said cheerfully.

It wasn't good news. Bryan's hours at the rink were the only time Ivy felt as if she could let down her guard.

"What are your symptoms?" Kelsey asked.

"I get a little confused."

"A little! Uncle Pat just about lost it," Max said, "when Bryan called him *Pete*."

"He thought I was faking it."

"Were you?" Ivy asked.

Bryan leaned forward and grinned at her. "What d'you think?"

Kelsey pulled him back. "I think that you remember what you want to." She rested her legs on his lap. "And you had better remember me. We've already had one convenient amnesiac this summer."

"Whoa! I hadn't thought about that!" Max said. "It's kind of eerie, two guys pulled out of the water off Chatham, both knocked silly. But at least you know who you are, Bryan."

Bryan glanced sideways at Ivy. "I do." Then he turned back to Kelsey. "What did you say your name was?"

She gave him a smack on his arm, and he and Max laughed.

Ivy studied Bryan. When Tristan had taken over Luke's dead body, Luke's mind and spirit had passed on completely. Tristan had had no access to the memories of Luke. So wouldn't Gregory have the same problem? But Gregory had been lurking about since the night of the séance, so he'd had plenty of opportunity to learn things about Bryan. There'd be slip-ups here and there, of course, but he'd muddle through, especially with the excuse of a concussion. What exactly did Gregory know about Bryan's crimes? Enough to continue Bryan's threats against "Luke"?

"So guess where I'm going for vacation," Bryan said.

"You're leaving the Cape?" Kelsey asked, frowning.

"Leaving *my friends*?" Bryan grinned at Ivy. "No. I'm staying at Max's house and enjoying his toys."

And the perfect freedom that the situation would give him, Ivy thought, *with no restraints from Uncle Pat or the job.*

"Lucky me," said Max.

Bryan gave Kelsey a little push off the sofa. "Come on, let's roll, babe. I'm tired of sitting around."

"Just give me a minute to change my shirt."

"Meet us at the car," Bryan said, and tossed Max the keys. As Max exited, Bryan turned back. "Ivy," he said in a voice so soft and so close to her face that she half heard him, half read his lips. "Tell Tristan thanks for the tip."

"THE TIP?" LACEY ASKED, REPEATING IVY'S WORDS.

Tristan said nothing. He had given up trying to reach Lacey earlier that evening and was a little annoyed when the angel showed up immediately after being called by Ivy. The three of them sat at a large dining table in front of a set of sliding doors at the Steadmans' summer home. The light of a round moon silvered the deck outside, and beyond that, whitened the meadow of sea grass. Ivy had opened the sliding door and pulled the vertical blinds back a few inches to let in a salty breeze.

"What was he talking about?" Ivy asked. "Did Gregory come here?"

Lacey's eyes widened. "He came and you told him who you were?"

Tristan felt cornered; he knew they weren't going to like his answer. "I went to Chase's house Sunday night."

"Tristan!" Ivy chided.

"I can't sit here and do nothing, Ivy! I promised Philip I'd take care of you."

Lacey jumped in quickly: "Don't blame Philip. You know what's at stake."

For Tristan, the only thing at stake was losing Ivy. "At first," he said, "Gregory didn't know who I was. He tried to take over my mind."

"Then he realized he was up against something not quite human," Lacey guessed.

Tristan nodded.

Lacey turned to Ivy. "This is getting scary."

"No," Tristan argued, "it's getting better. With both of us trapped in a body, it levels the playing field."

Lacey looked at him as if he was crazy. "What—you think this is some kind of sport?"

"The thing is, Tristan," Ivy said, "you were *placed* in

Luke's body. But Gregory managed to do this on his own."

"Exactly," Lacey declared. "Which means he is gaining dangerous powers."

Tristan shook his head. "Gregory's not that smart or that powerful. He hears the same voices as I do. The voices must have told him how."

"Let me get this straight," Lacey said. "You're feeling all upbeat and confident because the voices, which told a demon how to do something that only God is supposed to do, also have a hotline to you!"

Tristan pushed back from the table. He wasn't afraid—it was time to act. "The fact that Gregory is now inside Bryan makes it easy for me," he said, standing in front of the double doors, gazing out at the tall grasses and the sea beyond them. "Now, finally, destroying Gregory will mean simply killing a murderer."

"No!" Lacey cried. "Destroying Gregory will mean destroying yourself. It doesn't matter what he or Bryan has done. If you kill him, you'll damn your own soul."

Tristan saw Ivy close her eyes. In the moonlight she looked pale. "Tristan," she said, her voice quavering, "the goal is not to destroy Gregory. The goal is for you and me to be together."

Don't you see? Tristan wanted to shout at her. *Gregory will never allow that!* But for a moment she looked so fragile, worn thin by fear.

He sat down and reached across the table, taking her hand in his. "Okay, so let's try your plan. Let's find the evidence to pin Bryan's murders on him and put Gregory in jail for life. Let's help him write his own death sentence."

He felt Ivy's hand relax in his.

"Now you're thinking!" Lacey said.

He was thinking that it was worth a try—but if Gregory took one step too close to Ivy, nothing would stop Tristan from killing him.

Ten

"IT'S A SECRET FORMULA," WILL TOLD IVY ON Wednesday evening, as he brushed barbecue sauce onto chicken thighs and wings.

"A secret that comes in a bottle," Beth added, smiling. She was sitting sideways on the yard swing, filling up a notebook, her words spilling over in lines of various lengths—poetry.

Will grinned. "It's what I add to the bottle's ingredients that's the secret."

"Smells good," Ivy replied, dropping a bundle of

silverware on the scrubbed wood table and anchoring a pile of napkins with a rock. "Where's Kelsey going tonight?"

"To Wellfleet with Max and Bryan," Beth said.

"You can't watch over her every minute of the day," Will added, as if guessing Ivy's thoughts.

She nodded. As long as Kelsey was around other people, she'd be okay. But of course it was impossible to keep her and Bryan from being alone together.

Ivy turned back to the cottage to fetch a pitcher of iced tea. "Hey, Chase!" she called, catching sight of him coming down the path.

"Chase, how's it going?" Will asked.

"Fine." He barely looked at them. "I assume Dhanya's inside."

"Getting dressed," Beth said. "It's good to see you, Chase. I was really worried about you."

"No reason to be."

"There was enough reason to keep you overnight in the hospital," Will observed. "What did they test you for?"

Chase gave him a cool stare. "The usual things when you strike your head on the edge of a boat. Max nearly killed us all."

"Chase," Ivy said quietly, "you were driving when the boat turned over. And afterward, when Max rescued you, you were barely conscious."

Chase glanced away.

"Do you remember that?" she asked curiously.

"How can I, if I was unconscious? They said I had a seizure."

"A seizure," Ivy repeated. It made sense. Historians thought that many people who had been labeled "possessed by the devil" actually suffered from epilepsy. The explanation could just as easily work in reverse. And to someone like Chase, for whom control and mental superiority were everything, a physiological explanation would be more agreeable than the idea of a demon taking over his mind. "Well, that can be managed with medication."

"I'm not taking it. There's nothing wrong with me."

"Hey, Chase," Dhanya said, opening the screen door. "Sorry—couldn't decide what to wear." Coming to stand next to him, she reached up and gently touched his face. "How are you?"

He pulled away from her as if he couldn't stand someone touching his head. "Let's go."

Ivy watched as he and Dhanya walked toward the path to the parking lot. Dhanya tried to take his hand, but he let her fingers slip through his.

Will returned to his grilling. "What a jerk, blaming the accident on the guy who saved his life."

"Go easy on him, Will," Beth said. "He's experienced something he can't understand. And he's so alone."

Will grimaced. "If he stopped imagining himself

mentally superior to the rest of us, maybe he'd have some company."

"His ego does make it harder for him than it has to be," Ivy said. "Still, I feel bad for Chase. He's really scared."

Will met Ivy's eyes. "So are the rest of us."

"TOMORROW'S MY DAY OFF," IVY SAID WHEN SHE called Tristan that night.

"Hey, guess what?" he replied. "It's my day off too. How about a date?"

"How about one away from the Cape—Providence."

"Does this mean I have a hot date with Gemma?"

Ivy laughed. Tristan was referring to her disguise as an art student and classmate of Corinne's.

"She can't wait to see you!"

They set a pickup time and place, Ice House Pond, then Ivy slipped her phone in her pocket and sat down to work on the coffee table puzzle. For a while Dusty slept soundly on the sofa next to her, then yawned, stretched his tufted toes, and leaped to the floor with a heavy thump. Standing at the cottage door, he meowed, impatient to begin his twilight hunt.

When Ivy let out the Maine coon, she was surprised to see Max sitting in a lawn chair, drumming his fingers nervously on its flat wood arms. Hearing the screen door open, he turned.

"Hey, Max. Are you waiting for someone?"

"I'm getting my nerve up."

"I'm sorry, Dhanya's out."

"I came to see you."

Ivy tried to read his face in the shadows. Did he sense that something was different about Bryan? Maybe her questions at the party had made him remember something useful to her. "Come on in."

After accepting her offer of a raspberry iced tea, he sat on the sofa, staring down at the puzzle. He propped his right foot on his left knee, then changed his mind and propped his left foot on his right knee.

"So what's up?" Ivy asked, handing him the cold bottle, sitting on the chair at a right angle to him.

He played with the sole of his boat shoe. "We're friends. At least, I think of you as a friend."

"We are," Ivy said, and waited.

"Friends should be honest with each other."

Ivy nodded.

"I almost killed you."

"What?!" she exclaimed.

"I almost killed you," he repeated. "It was some miracle that I didn't."

Ivy stared at him. "Max, what happened on the boat wasn't your fault."

"No," he said, "not that. Your car accident."

Ivy blinked, stunned into silence.

"The night you and Beth came to my house to pick up Dhanya and Kelsey. I drove you off the road."

"*You* did that?" Her voice cracked with emotion. "Why?"

He shook his head, as if he didn't know what more to say, then rose and started pacing the room. "I didn't *try* to do it. I tried *not* to hit you—that part I remember clearly. But I also remember my car going straight toward yours. So maybe I didn't try until it was too late.

"I guess I was drunk. But the thing is, I don't actually remember drinking. I remember that my party was getting out of hand, everyone boozing too much. I looked for Bryan, because he's good at calming things down. He wasn't around, so I left, just to drive around a while and get away from it all. On my way back, I guess I was driving too fast and—and it happened."

He stopped his pacing and turned to look at her. It was nearly dark inside the cottage. Ivy reached and turned on the lamp. Max looked as confused as she felt.

"Why didn't you slow down?" she asked. "Why didn't you move over to the right side of the road?"

"I tried to. I mean, I *thought* I did. But I couldn't control the car. I was pulling on the steering wheel as hard as I could, but it wouldn't turn—it just wouldn't! My car just kept going toward you, until you pulled sideways and flipped over."

Ivy sat back against the chair cushion, thinking.

"After you did, I rushed away," Max said. He sat down on the chair across from her and dropped his head for a moment. "I'm ashamed of myself. I should have stopped. It was close to my house, and I kept telling myself the kids at the party would hear the crash—they'd help you. I parked on the other side of the causeway, then ran back, got there the same time as the emergency vehicles. I was a coward."

Ivy didn't speak for a minute. The part of her that had grown fond of Max wanted to say it was no longer important; she and Beth were fine. But another part of her knew that Max had been as wrong as Bryan, abandoning his victims after a hit-and-run. Good people were also capable of doing very bad things.

"Max, I blame you for running, but for nothing else. I believe you tried to avoid my car. You aren't the kind of person to deliberately hurt another. Besides," she added, "for your own safety, you'd have turned your car aside."

"But the thing is, I didn't."

Because Gregory wouldn't let him, Ivy thought. Gregory had already come into the world through the séance, and he saw his chance to kill her. He didn't care if he killed Max as well. Max had fought for control of the wheel, but Gregory was stronger and had succeeded—except that Tristan then stepped in and kissed her.

She couldn't imagine how to explain this to Max.

"Something was wrong with your car. There's no way you would have deliberately done that."

"I don't want to make excuses, Ivy. I want to admit I did something terrible and have it over with."

"Why didn't you admit it then?" she asked curiously. "Maybe not right away, but a few days later?"

"The night of the party—two or three in the morning—Bryan came back. I told him what had happened. He said to wait, just wait, let everything calm down. Then, when we found out you and Beth were okay, he said a confession would only screw things up. My parents would get upset. The police would start investigating my parties and asking a lot of nosy questions."

Like where Bryan was that night, Ivy thought.

"He said Dhanya would never want anything to do with me. So I put it off, and the longer I did, and the nicer you were to me, the harder it got." He stood up and walked to the screen door, gazing out for a moment. "Then the boat trip happened."

"What about it?"

"It was the same feeling as when I was driving toward you. When Chase grabbed the wheel and I couldn't get back control, it was like it was happening all over again."

Because it was, Ivy thought. Gregory was in charge again. But Gregory had known that she was wearing a life vest. This time, Ivy realized, he wasn't aiming for her, but for a body of his own—the perfect body for him, a match made in hell.

"Last night," Max went on, "I kept dreaming about your accident. When I woke up this morning, I knew I had to come clean."

"Did you tell Bryan you were going to confess?" Ivy asked. "He's staying at your house now, isn't he?"

Max returned to the chair across from her. "I told him about the nightmare. I didn't say that I was going to talk to you, because I knew I was cowardly enough to let him talk me out of it."

"There's no need to tell him now," Ivy said. The less Gregory knew about Max's affairs, the less power Gregory would have over him.

"Do you forgive me?"

She saw the dampness in the corners of his eyes. "Max, we all make mistakes—"

"And then act like we didn't, even when someone could have died?" He looked away from her.

"We're human. We make mistakes, and sometimes we're afraid enough to cover them up."

"Will you say it?" Max asked. "It would help me to hear you say it."

She didn't want to forgive something caused by Gregory.

"Otherwise I feel like I can't get free of it," Max

explained. "I guess that's selfish, but I feel like I can't—"

"I forgive you," Ivy said, wondering if her heart could ever truly forgive Gregory. "I want to be free of it too."

After Max left, Ivy sat staring at the puzzle, pushing pieces around, trying to make connections. She forced two pieces together, then had to undo them.

If Gregory was responsible for killing her, wasn't Tristan justified in bringing her back to life? Hadn't Tristan's kiss of life set things right again? Right—according to whom? Right, if she was supposed to stay alive on this earth. Right, if their desire to be together in this world was the only thing that mattered.

Ivy wanted to believe that Tristan and Max were victims of Gregory's evil, forced into doing the wrong thing. But Max's situation had made clear in her mind an important distinction: While Max wasn't the one who drove her off the road, he had made the wrong choice in how he responded to the accident. When he left her and Beth to die, Max had succumbed to a temptation created by Gregory. Like Max, Tristan had faced a great temptation created by Gregory. Now he was stripped of his angelic powers, and the temptation to protect her was even stronger. The truth was that each person was responsible for how he or she responded to a situation.

In her heart, Ivy knew that Tristan's mission was to

save his fallen soul. She would do anything to help him—
anything! But she feared that the best thing for Tristan
was for her to stay out of his way. It was the hardest way
to love.

Eleven

THE MORNING MIST STILL CLUNG TO THE TREES SUR-
rounding Ice House Pond. Tristan hoped his borrowed
clothes, faded jeans and a khaki T-shirt, helped him blend
in. He hummed to himself as he walked, feeling as if he had
been given a furlough from prison. A few minutes later, Ivy's
VW pulled up. He got in quickly and slid down in the seat.
She squeezed his hand and continued driving: The sooner
they got away from Orleans, the better. They didn't talk
until the car was speeding along the Mid-Cape Highway.

"I'm disappointed," he said. "Where's Gemma?"

Ivy grinned. "We're meeting her at the Dunkin' Donuts on the other side of the canal. She's been looking forward to seeing you, too! "

"So who are we visiting this time?"

"Luke's former landlady, Crystal Abbot. In one of the news articles, it said the police interviewed her, but people don't always tell the police everything they know. She refused to talk to reporters. Maybe she'll talk to *Luke*. It's worth a try."

"It's worth it just to sit next to you," Tristan said. With his arm outstretched, he dropped his head back against the headrest. Laying his wrist on her shoulder, he let his fingers nestle in her hair. "I wish we could drive like this straight across the country."

Ivy didn't reply. When he turned his head, he saw her biting her lip.

"We have today," he said quietly. "It's more than we once thought we'd have."

During their stop at Dunkin' Donuts, they started laughing again. Ivy emerged from the restroom wearing sheer leggings colored with hearts, roses, and skulls, and a pair of laced-up booties that ended in open-toed thongs. Over her tank top she wore her prize purchase from a Provincetown shop, a vest woven from ribbons and pieces of glass, the recycled mouths of beer bottles. Her usually gold eyelashes looked as if they'd been tarred.

"I don't know how you can keep your eyelids up," Tristan remarked as they walked to the car, his arm around her. He could feel her giggling.

Since they didn't want to leave an electronic trail via her GPS, Ivy had printed out a map and marked on it Mrs. Abbot's address. They reached the Providence neighborhood of River Gardens close to nine o'clock and parked across the street from the tall frame home. In a neighborhood of rusty chain-link fences, Mrs. Abbot's yard seemed more welcoming than the others with its assortment of plastic toys. Flowers grew at the corners of her chipped concrete steps. Next to the door were two buttons and two mailboxes. Ivy pushed the bell marked ABBOT.

The door cracked opened and the face of a little boy appeared in the three inches between the frame and the door. "Mom said the apartment's rented."

"We're not here for an apartment," Ivy began to explain.

The door closed, then just as quickly opened wide and the child flew out. Footsteps sounded in the hallway and a blur of a little girl raced past Ivy and Tristan.

"Zeke, I'm gonna hammer you!" she cried. Chasing the boy, she left the door gaping.

"Hello?" Tristan called as he and Ivy stepped inside.

At the end of the hall, tucked beneath the stairway, another door was open and a baby crawled toward them. A pair of strong arms appeared, scooping up the child.

"Sorry," the woman said, moving into the hallway, the struggling baby in her arms. "The apartment is leased now."

Tristan removed his baseball cap and sunglasses.

"Luke! So it's true. You *have* been coming back to the Gardens."

He simply nodded, not knowing what Luke had called his landlady.

"Hello, Mrs. Abbot," Ivy said.

"Crystal," she replied with a nod. The full-bodied woman had mahogany-colored skin and close-cropped hair. Her pleasant face was set off by a huge pair of hoop earrings.

"Crystal, this is my friend Gemma."

"A friend through Corinne," Ivy added. "Corinne and I went to art school together."

The woman smiled a little, eyeing Ivy's outfit. "Should've guessed," she said. "Come in. Watch the scooter. And the skates."

The Abbots' living room was sunny, its furniture worn, and its scatter rugs truly scattered, creating the feeling of kids rushing through it even in the silence. Crystal balanced the baby on her hip and picked pillows off the floor with her free hand as she led them through the room to the kitchen.

"Al's asleep. My husband works the night shift," she added, directing that explanation at "Gemma."

They followed the landlady onto a porch with two rockers. Tristan sat on the steps. The backyard was a small jungle of weed trees growing under one large tree. But, judging by the ropes and tires tied to the big tree and the open bins of leftover construction materials, it was a kid's paradise. The boy and girl were busy stringing up a tent.

"Just like old times," Crystal said, and Tristan smiled, feeling that same awkwardness and humility he had felt before when people who cared for Luke looked fondly at him.

"Better put on your sunglasses and hat. I'm not telling the kids it's you. Don't want them saying something to the wrong person."

He nodded and did as she said.

"Whoever the wrong person is," Crystal added, frowning. "Do you know who killed Corinne?"

"No."

Crystal rocked a moment, then turned to Ivy. "Do you think the murderer was someone from Corinne's new life? Did she make enemies at art school?"

"She didn't make many friends."

The baby started fussing, and to Tristan's amazement, Crystal handed the child to him. "Micah always liked you."

Tristan looked at Ivy, feeling helpless. He tried to remember how he'd seen people hold babies. The little bare feet kept beating against Tristan's legs, so he held the kid by his armpits, standing him up so he could flex his pudgy knees. "You're getting big, buddy."

The baby grabbed the brim of Tristan's hat and started chewing on it. "Whoa! You don't know where that's been," Tristan said, holding the child with one hand and turning his hat backward. Micah grabbed Tristan's sunglasses and started swinging them around, batting him on the side of the head, then dropped the glasses and collapsed against Tristan's chest. His small body was damp and warm and smelled like powder. Patting the baby's back, hoping he wasn't going to spit up, Tristan glanced over his shoulder and saw Ivy laughing.

"You should have gone west, Luke," Crystal said. "Or south. The Cape's not far enough."

"Yeah, I know that now."

"What happened to Alicia? That girl wasn't suicidal."

"I agree," he said.

"I heard talk, blaming it on you," she continued. "I know that's not true."

"I think the person who killed Corinne also killed her. She was here with me the night Corinne asked me to meet her at Four Winds. Alicia didn't realize it when it happened, but she was my alibi."

"So they killed your alibi." Crystal closed her eyes for a moment. "God have mercy."

"Did you see Alicia that night?" Ivy asked Crystal. "I

know if you had seen what time she left, you would've told that to the police. But maybe, at least, you saw her arrive." Ivy's voice pleaded. "Anything that you could tell them now might help."

Crystal glanced at "Luke."

"You always could win over the girls' hearts." Then she pointed to a set of exterior steps. "That's the stairway to the third floor," she told Ivy. "Evenings are noisy here—Al gets the kids wound up. I hole up in the bedroom and study. I didn't see or hear anything. I told that to the police when they came banging on our door at two a.m. I wasn't awake enough to think about giving anyone an alibi. The best I could do was keep them from searching Luke's place until they had a warrant."

So, another dead end, thought Tristan.

"How about Bryan Sweeney?" Ivy asked, and let the question hang, as if testing the landlady's gut response to the mention of him.

Crystal watched her kids wheeling a cinderblock to the tent in a rusty wheelbarrow. "Bryan was a help. He got Luke out of here. But he and I, we don't get along. You know that, Luke."

"Why not?" Ivy asked.

"You know him?" the woman asked back. "He's a lot like Corinne. Ambitious. Self-centered. He disguises it bet-ter than Corinne did, but he was always looking out for himself." Crystal studied Ivy, then rose to her feet as if she had made some decision. "I've kept something for you, Luke. I guess I can give it to you in front of your friend here."

She disappeared into the kitchen, and Ivy and Tristan exchanged hopeful glances. The baby straightened his chubby legs, straining to see where his mother had gone, then rested back against Tristan's shoulder.

Crystal returned carrying a cereal box. Slipping her finger under the cardboard flap, she pulled out a small padded envelope and handed it to Tristan in exchange for the baby. The envelope, addressed to Luke, had a handwritten return address for Corinne Santori.

"It arrived two days after Corinne was murdered, one day after the police searched your rooms."

Tristan looked up questioningly at Crystal.

"Al and I decided not to tell them. If they had caught you, I would have found a way to get it to you. As far as we were concerned, it was for your eyes only."

It took all of Tristan's self-discipline not to rip the package open. He tried to loosen the packing tape, then asked for a pair of scissors. With a few snips, he eased open one end of the envelope. Something small and solid fell out.

"Her flash drive!" Ivy exclaimed softly.

Tristan set the drive on the porch floor next to him, then pulled out a note.

"Luke, keep this safe for me," he read aloud.

"What's the postmark on the envelope?" Ivy asked.

Tristan squinted. "The day before she died."

"Somebody was breathing down her neck," Crystal said.

Tristan picked up the flash drive. Somewhere in these 16 gigs were pictures of Bryan's damaged car. Those photos, Corinne's note, and the photo of Bryan wearing the cufflinks matching the one left next to his first victim would be enough evidence to convince the police.

"I wouldn't advertise you've got that," Crystal advised. "Corinne was always poking her camera into other people's business. There'll be plenty of folks desperate enough to pry it out of your hands."

Tristan smiled up at her, then pocketed the drive. Of course! There would be others who had done lesser things than murder, who could verify that Corinne was a blackmailer. They wouldn't have come forward willingly, but if evidence was presented now, they'd have to talk to police. "Do you have something we can put this envelope in?"

Crystal brought him a zip-lock bag.

"I—I don't know how to thank you for this," Tristan said.

"You could pay your last two months of rent," Crystal replied.

"I owed you two months?" Tristan saw Ivy bite back her laughter.

"You paid off the third month by painting the bathrooms, remember?"

"Write down the amount," Ivy said. "You'll get it."

Crystal did, then walked them to the front door with Micah on her hip.

Tristan debated how to say good-bye. A handshake seemed too formal for a woman Luke used to sit on the back porch with. But each hug he gave while playing the role of Luke made him feel more dishonest. He laid his hand gently on the baby's head. "Soon," he said, "you'll be chasing your big brother and sister. You'll be showing them just how fast those little feet can go."

Crystal's dark eyes shimmered. "We miss you, Luke."

As they drove away, Ivy smiled. "A natural," she teased. "Who'd have thought it? I was waiting to see you feed and change him."

"Yeah, and tape his diaper to his undershirt. Did you see how little his undershirt was? Did you see his miniature fingernails?"

Ivy laughed at Tristan.

They had taken Ivy's laptop from the trunk, and Tristan booted it up as she drove, then slipped in the flash drive. "I'm making a backup."

"I've been trying to think of a good place for us to plug in and start searching the files. I checked online last night. With Alicia's death, you've resurfaced as a news story in

Massachusetts and Rhode Island, complete with photos."

"Yes, but according to Chase, they're not very flattering," Tristan joked. His heart felt so much lighter now. "How about Connecticut? Hartford. It's easier to be overlooked in a city."

"Good idea! I know exactly where we'd blend in."

Two hours and one rest stop later, during which Ivy shed everything of Gemma's except the darkened eyelashes, she pulled into a parking lot belonging to Trinity University. Tristan placed the laptop in the protective pocket of her knapsack and slung it over his shoulder. Hand in hand, they walked the path to the library. They could have been any two college kids on the half-empty summer campus.

For the next several hours they looked at photos. At first glance, they had thought their task might be easy. Though the drive held a huge number of photos and there were folders within folders, the files were named in a systematic way that a compulsive artist—or competent blackmailer— might label them.

But promising names of folders yielded useless files. In a folder labeled RIVER GARDENS there was just one car, which appeared in a photo of Corinne's stepfather and the car he drove for hire. They found her photo essay, *Carscape*, among her schoolwork, but those photos were so artistically rendered there was no shot of an easily identifiable car with front-end damage.

"I don't know enough about how a photographer would use a computer," Tristan said, sitting back in his chair. "Is there a way of accessing the photos according to date?"

"The date they were taken?" Ivy sighed. "I don't know."

"If she sent this to Luke for safekeeping, it's *got* to have something incriminating."

"I agree." Ivy rubbed her eyes and sat back in her chair. "Perhaps Corinne used a large drive and put this many photos on it to keep anyone who got ahold of it from being able to easily find the incriminating photos. Tristan, what about letting Will have a crack at this? He does a lot of artwork on his Mac, including photography. He'd know the kinds of tech things Corinne knew. And being visual, he might see a pattern in the photos that we don't."

Tristan nodded. "Let's take a break, then look a little more. If we don't find anything, we'll turn it over to him."

They found lunch at a campus café called the Cave and carried their sandwiches out to the main quad for a picnic beneath a tree. A scattering of girls sunbathed on the grass. A guy and his dog played with a Frisbee. Summer students strolled along a flagstone walk that ran past a block of connected brownstone buildings. The buildings' steep roofs were punctuated by gables, towers, and dormers, so perfect in its college-Gothic detail, it looked like a movie set.

After finishing his sandwich, Tristan lay back in the grass, gazing up at the canopy of maple leaves and the small petals of blue sky peeking through here and there. Ivy lay close to him, resting her head on his shoulder. He twined her hair lightly around his finger and listened to a fragment of conversation as two people passed by, a younger guy talking excitedly about something he'd read, and an older man, whose contribution was simply a chuckle.

"This is where you'll be going to college," Tristan said suddenly. Earlier he had noticed that Ivy had seemed to know her way to the library. In a short month, she would come here to study, live in a dorm, and make friends with people who occupied a world far different from the one he could inhabit as Luke.

Ivy raised her head and gazed down at him. "What is it? What are you thinking about?"

As Luke, he didn't have a high school diploma, a home, or a job; and he didn't have the money or track record to get those things. "Andrew and Maggie, and your new college friends—they're not going to be raising a glass of champagne to you and me. Ivy, nobody who loves you will want us to be together."

"Philip will. And Beth and Will—they're glad for us," she argued.

"To everyone else, I'll always be a suspect who fled the police."

"It doesn't matter. I know who you are. I knew it before you did."

"If we get *lucky*," Tristan continued, "I'll be seen as the best friend of a murderer, the old boyfriend of a black-mailer, and—"

She touched his lips with her finger, silencing him. "All that matters is what you are to me."

"What I am to you is *fallen*."

She put her arms around him. "You'll redeem yourself. We'll figure it out."

But all he could see were the worldly things that would keep him and Ivy apart, realities he didn't know how to change. The one thing he knew he could do was protect her from Gregory. It would be worth his soul!

"You're still you, Tristan. And I will love you always."

He kissed her. God help him—he knew he'd give her the kiss of life again! "Even after—"

She cradled his head in her arms. "*Ever*after."

"SO, CAN YOU HELP US, WILL?" IVY ASKED LATE Thursday night.

Will had sat quietly in his straight-backed chair, toying with pieces of colored chalk that were scattered on the table next to him, listening to Ivy's story. The picture he'd been working on when she entered his room had been hastily slipped beneath a course catalog for NYU.

He dropped the chalk and turned to her. "Incredible. I don't think I could survive all you and Tristan have gone through."

"I know your heart, Will. You could. But I hope you never have to."

He took a deep breath and let it out slowly, as if he was still working through the things she had told him about Bryan and the murder investigations, then he held out his hand for the flash drive. "Let me see what I can find. If Corinne was serious about hiding things, it's going to take some time. I'll copy this. You should put Corinne's in a safe-deposit box."

"Good idea."

He slipped the USB drive into the computer's slot, clicked on the icon, and began opening the folders. "Oh, wow!"

"I know I'm dumping a lot on you."

He turned to smile at her. "Hey, a chance to snoop around the work of another artist—an artist and blackmailer—I'm going to enjoy this!" His voice was light, but his dark eyes showed an intensity and concern that betrayed his smile.

"Thank you, Will." Ivy handed him a folder stuffed with photos and articles she had printed from the Internet, as well as a list of names and physical descriptions of the people and places she had visited in River Gardens, material that might help Will identify what he was seeing in the photographs.

Slipping Corinne's USB drive in her pocket, she said, "Will, by telling you all this, I'm putting you in some danger. What do you think we ought to do about Beth?"

"She'd want to know," he said without hesitation. "I can fill her in."

Ivy nodded in agreement, then rose to leave. At the door she turned back. "By the way, that's an awesome picture of Beth beneath your course catalog. You ought to show her."

Will's tan got a little pinker.

On the way back from Will's room, Ivy met up with Dhanya. Her roommate was singing to herself and swinging her purse as she walked toward the cottage door. She stopped and smiled at Ivy. "Hey."

"Hey, Dhanya. Did you have fun with Max?"

"Actually, yes," Dhanya replied. "When he asked me out, I just wanted to get away from here and stop worrying about how weird Chase has been acting. But the glass at the Sandwich Museum was fabulous. Afterward we walked around the town. Max is good about shopping—doesn't hurry me at all. You know, sometimes even my mother gets frustrated when I shop, but Max is very patient."

"Yeah?" Knowing what it was like to grocery shop with her roommate, Ivy could easily imagine Dhanya picking up piece after piece of merchandise unaware, as she admired it, how happy Max was admiring her.

"He asked if I'd like to go to Nantucket for my day off. He said it's really nice there." She peeked at Ivy, as if wanting an opinion.

"It's supposed to be great," Ivy said, commenting on the island rather than Max. Dhanya needed to decide for herself who she wanted to hang around with. Ivy held open the screen door, but Dhanya stopped on the cottage steps, as if she wanted to say something more.

"You know, it was Max who saved Chase when he was having the seizure," Dhanya said. "Despite all the times Chase has made fun of Max, Max doesn't say anything mean about him, and he doesn't go around saying he saved him."

"I know."

Dhanya slipped her phone from her pocket and smiled a little self-consciously. "Think I'll text Max—just so he doesn't make other plans."

Ivy smiled to herself. What other plans could he possibly want to make!

Twelve

"KEL-SEY!" BRYAN HOLLERED FROM THE LIVING ROOM Friday evening.

Ivy laid her bag of music books on the kitchen chair and glanced toward the front door, where Bryan had let himself in.

"I'm up here," Kelsey yelled from the bedroom. "Come on up."

"No, stay where you are! I'm not dressed," Dhanya called down, prompting loud laughter from Kelsey.

A moment later, Bryan appeared in the doorway between

the living room and kitchen. "Hello, Ivy." His low, seductive tone made Ivy's skin creep. It felt as if they were back in the kitchen in Stonehill, when Gregory was alive in his own body.

"Hi." She made herself busy, rinsing and filling her water bottle.

He picked up her bag of books, sat in the chair, and started paging through her music. She wanted to snatch it out of his hands, but resisted the impulse, not wanting him to know he unnerved her. Opening the freezer, she grabbed some ice cubes and plunked them in her bottle.

"Want to come to the movie tonight?" he asked.

"What are you seeing?"

"*Harvest Moon*. It's about a serial killer."

"How refreshing. Where's Max?"

"Said he had some kind of errand to do, but I don't think he likes violent movies." Bryan crossed the kitchen to Ivy. "Some people are frightened by fiction and their own dark imaginings," he said, moving his mouth close to her ear, "and others, by the real thing."

The footsteps on the stairway alerted them, but Bryan took his time moving away. Kelsey rewarded him with a scathing glance at Ivy. "Thank you for entertaining my boyfriend, but I'm here now."

"I was just fixing myself something to drink," Ivy replied.

Bryan flashed Kelsey a boyish grin. "Thirsty, babe? I've got a case of beer in the car."

"Great!" Kelsey replied.

"Remember the party," Ivy said, unable to warn Kelsey in a more direct way about Bryan. "Remember how sick you felt."

"Which party was that?" Kelsey asked, grinning, then stuck her head in the stairwell. "Hurry up, Dhanya!"

"Dhanya's going?" Ivy asked, surprised.

"Kels, can I borrow your blue sweater?" Dhanya called back.

"If you get your sweet bum down here before the movie's half over, yes."

Ivy didn't like the idea of demonic Bryan driving Kelsey and Dhanya around, and all the excuses a case of beer could provide. "Actually, I would like to go."

Kelsey frowned. "I thought you were going to practice piano."

"I'll do it Sunday."

Kelsey made a face. "Isn't Father What's-His-Name going to be disappointed?"

"Lighten up, Kelsey," Bryan intervened. "It's Friday night, and Ivy needs a break. Some murder and mayhem might do her good."

"I'm ready," Ivy said, picking up her purse.

Twenty minutes later they arrived at the theater, which had been built long before the day of multiplexes. Drafts of musty air-conditioning and the heavy smell of buttered popcorn wafted down the aisle. Its seats were so worn, Ivy could feel the metal frame through the cushions. Kelsey made sure that Bryan entered the row first, followed by herself, then Dhanya. Ivy was glad to be three people away from Bryan.

"I hope there's not a lot of blood," Dhanya said. "I don't mind serial killers as long as they don't get gory."

"You prefer murderers who strangle?" Bryan asked her, tipping his head far enough forward to look at Ivy.

"I prefer killers who do anything other than make people bleed."

"My feelings exactly," he said. "Who wants to clean that up?"

There was only one scene with blood, the rest of the plot being devoted to profiling the serial killer who "harvested" every full moon. Ivy liked psychological thrillers, but she struggled to follow this one. Her mind felt unable to process what she was seeing and hearing. When the movie ended much sooner than expected, she wondered if she had nodded off. As the house lights came up and the credits flew by, Ivy turned to Dhanya and found her roommate asleep.

"Dhanya? Dhanya," she said quietly.

In the dimly lit theater, she could see Dhanya's eyes darting back and forth beneath her lids. Ivy nudged her. "Hey, you."

Bryan leaned across Kelsey. "Dhanya, wake up," he commanded.

She opened her eyes and glanced around quickly, as if trying to figure out where she was, then visibly sagged with relief.

"You were dreaming," Ivy told her. "Everything's okay."

Dhanya searched Ivy's face, her dark eyes troubled.

"What is it?" Ivy asked.

Bryan leaned across Kelsey. "Something wrong, Dhanya?"

"No." But her fingers were curled tightly in her lap.

"Bad dream?" he persisted. "Tell me about it."

His eagerness for her to recount the dream sounded a warning bell in Ivy's mind. "Let's go to the lobby, where the lights are brighter," she said to her roommate. "You'll feel better."

But Dhanya stayed in her seat. "It was so real. The dream *felt* so real, Ivy. I was on the train bridge. You were there too. And Luke. You were standing with Luke."

Dhanya's brow knit, then she quickly glanced away from Ivy.

"Go on," Bryan encouraged softly.

"The girl who died was also there. Alicia."

Ivy's heart beat faster.

"And?" Bryan prompted.

"Luke and—" Dhanya ducked her head and swallowed the words.

"Spit it out!" Kelsey said.

"—pushed her off the bridge."

"Luke and *Ivy* pushed Alicia off the bridge?" Bryan asked.

"It was just a dream, I know that," Dhanya said quickly.

But she was haunted by the dream—Ivy could see it in her eyes. The vision had been that powerful. Had Gregory learned how to project ideas and images to someone sitting close to him?

"I don't know about the rest of you," Kelsey interjected, "but these chairs are making my butt hurt."

Ivy stood up and Dhanya followed, but when Ivy reached back to put an arm around her, Dhanya pulled away. She looked both apologetic and confused. Folding her arms and hunching her shoulders as if she was cold, she walked alone up the aisle.

Bryan smiled and put his arm around Kelsey. The gleam of satisfaction in his eyes chilled Ivy's soul.

TRISTAN WAS DEEP INTO A JOHN GRISHAM NOVEL, sitting in the big leather chair in the living room, only his clip-on reading light shining on the book's yellow pages, when he heard the sharp knock at the front door. Clicking off the tiny light, he waited. A second knock brought him to his feet. He quietly climbed the stairs and stood at the window above the front door, separating the slats of the blinds with his fingers.

He expected to see Bryan, Chase—or worse, the police. What he saw was a guy of smaller stature wearing a bright print shirt. *Max?* The visitor fit Ivy's description of him.

As far as Tristan knew, Bryan had kept his River Gardens life separate from his college life, so Tristan guessed that there had been little or no contact between Max and the real Luke. But Max, along with the others, would have seen him at the carnival last month, when Alicia "recognized" him.

The guy at the door took several steps back from the house, surveying the windows. Tristan quickly let go of the blind. If he answered the door, it would confirm that he was holing up here. Of course, not answering the door would hardly prove otherwise.

"Luke?" the visitor called softly. "It's Max Moyer, a friend of Bryan's. I have to talk to you."

A trap?

"I need to talk about the night you almost drowned."

Tristan headed downstairs. If this was bait, he couldn't turn away from it.

When he opened the door, Max looked relieved. "Can I come in?"

Tristan gestured, then quickly closed the door behind him. "I keep the lights off." There was no reason to admit that he watched videos and used lanterns when Ivy came.

He knew the darkened house well and Max didn't; Tristan wanted to keep that advantage. "This way."

Max followed the sound of Tristan's footsteps to the family room, walking tentatively, bumping into an ottoman.

"There's a chair right behind that," Tristan told him, then sat down on the long sofa at an angle to Max's chair. "How'd you find me?"

"Put two and two together," Max replied. "Kelsey said Ivy's been sneaking off at night—walking and kayaking—so I figured you were somewhere close. Aunt Cindy was best friends with the people whose son was struck by lightning, and they left the Cape. I looked up the Steadmans' address, saw it was an easy paddle across the harbor, and thought I'd check it out."

Tristan nodded.

"The night you almost drowned," Max began, then hesitated. "What do you remember about it?"

"A lot more than I used to." For Tristan to say he remembered nothing would encourage lying. And he knew enough of what had happened to fake it. "What do *you* remember?" Tristan asked back.

"When I'm awake or when I'm asleep?"

Tristan tried to tease out the meaning of Max's response, then got up to open the blinds. He needed to see his face. Max blinked as if Tristan had turned on a bright light.

"A couple nights ago, I told Ivy that I was the one who drove her and Beth off the road."

"I know." Ivy had relayed that to him during their trip to River Gardens.

"That's what I remember during the day—every day—since it happened," Max said. "I could have killed her!"

Tristan remained silent.

"And you know what I did to you?"

Having no idea, Tristan repeated Max's earlier words: "The night I almost drowned."

"I tried to kill you."

Tristan sat up straight—this was nonsense. But he decided to play along to see where it led. "Why'd you do it?" he asked aloud.

"I don't know!" The words were spoken close to a wail. "I have no clue why I'd fight you or anyone else. I've never been a fighter. I guess drinking turned me into some kind of crazy person."

More likely, Tristan thought, his good friend Bryan had taken advantage of an alcoholic blackout, concocting this story and convincing Max, in case the police ever caught up with him.

Without blaming Bryan and endangering Max, Tristan had to set things straight. "Max, do you remember the day after?"

"How could I forget? My parents were pissed. The police and insurance people were swarming."

"I bet they were. It's a wonder they didn't ask you where you got all those bruises and cuts."

"What do you mean?" Max replied. "I didn't have any."

"You didn't?" Tristan rose to his feet. "Stand up."

Max faced him a bit reluctantly.

"Do you know what I looked like when they found me?" Tristan asked. "I had bruises on every part of my body—arms, legs, gut, jaw—deep bruises that took weeks to fade. Oh, and a nice slit across my throat."

Max flinched.

"And I'm what—about eight inches taller than you?" Tristan continued. "Are you saying you got away from our epic fight without a scratch?"

Max stared at Tristan. He clasped his head with both hands then sat down. "So it really was just a dream."

"Which," Tristan guessed, "is what you meant when you said there was something you remembered when you were asleep."

"The details were so real. I didn't see how my mind could make it all up. My memory of driving Ivy's car off the road is kind of jumbled in my head, me trying to turn the wheel, being afraid, thinking I was going to die—everything going too fast, then slow, unbelievably slow. But the dream wasn't like that memory. It was more real than everyday life."

"Because it was just a dream," Tristan said. "I know who tried to kill me. That part of my memory has come back."

"Who?" Max asked quickly.

Tristan shook his head, declining to respond. Even if he

could convince Max, even if Max's heart and soul could be trusted—and Tristan thought they probably could—Max's ability to keep a poker face could not.

"Why don't you go to the police?" Max asked.

"When the time is right," Tristan said. "Max, if you tell the police where I am before then, it will be very dangerous for me. You can't tell anyone, not even Ivy's roommates or Bryan. Until the real murderer is in police custody, anyone with knowledge about me will be at risk."

It was the best persuasion Tristan could muster to keep the situation quiet; Max seemed to care enough about others to be guided by this kind of warning.

Tristan rose to walk his visitor to the door. "If there's something else you want me to know, it's best to tell Ivy rather than come here again. She'll make sure I get the message." He opened the door and saw that the driveway was empty. "Where's your car?"

"A few streets over."

"Watch your back, Max. Trust no one but Ivy."

Max gazed at Tristan for a long moment, then nodded and left.

Tristan dropped down in a crouch and leaned back against the front door, taking deep breaths. How could this have happened? He doubted it was a random dream. But neither his soul nor Gregory's could leave the bodies in which they were trapped. Somehow Gregory had learned how to extend his mental powers beyond his body and invade Max's dreams.

In the silent house, Tristan heard the ominous murmuring. *Which way? Which way?*

The voices! Tristan thought. It was the voices that had taught Gregory. And they would teach him, too, if he dared to listen.

Thirteen

"TRISTAN, WHERE WERE YOU LAST NIGHT?" IVY ASKED, greeting him with a hug.

As soon as she had arrived home Friday, she'd called him but hadn't been able to reach him until after midnight. Over the phone, she had quickly told him about Dhanya's dream, and they had agreed to meet the next evening and ask for Lacey's advice.

Holding her close, Tristan didn't answer for a moment. Outside the Steadmans' house the sky was a pale mauve; inside, the twilight was deeper.

"I was walking . . . and thinking."

When he let her go, Ivy took a step back, studying his face, trying to read his mood.

"I'm sorry," he said. "I left my phone in the house."

Which meant, Ivy suspected, he had left the house upset about something.

"Well, that was foolish." Lacey's voice preceded her shimmer.

Tristan swung toward the angel. "This isn't a jail! I'm not letting Gregory or Bryan turn me into a prisoner."

"No need to," Lacey replied as she materialized in the foyer. "You've put yourself in your own prison—it just looks like a body." She turned to Ivy. "So what's up? You sounded worried last night."

Ivy led the way to the family room, waited for Tristan to sit down, then sat close to him on the sofa. Lacey dropped down in a chair with a footstool and listened to Ivy's account of the scene at the movie theater.

"Do you remember my nightmares after Gregory tried to kill me?"

"The dreams where you were driving through a storm, looking for a house? You climbed the steps to the front door," Tristan recalled. "And there was . . . a large window, but you couldn't see through it. Then you took a step closer"—his back stiffened as he remembered Ivy's terror—"and the glass exploded."

"You'd wake up screaming," Lacey added. "And good old Gregory was always there by your side."

"When Dhanya awoke, it was like that," Ivy told them, "the way he leaned over her, probing for details. He looks like Bryan, but sometimes—the way he speaks and uses his hands—I see Gregory as if he was alive in his own flesh."

Lacey wriggled her shoulders.

"Dhanya isn't Gregory's only target," Tristan told them. He recounted Max's visit.

"What's Gregory trying to do?" Ivy asked Lacey.

"*How* is he doing it—that's what we need to know," Tristan said.

"One thing's for sure, he's putting on a good show— one he wants you to watch, Ivy," Lacey added, "or he wouldn't have tried it in front of you." The angel tapped her fingernails on the table next to her. "Where does Gregory— Bryan—live?"

"With Max, ever since the boat accident," Ivy replied.

"So, first Gregory seeds a dream in a guy who is sound asleep, a guy he can stand right next to in the middle of the night. Then he tries it again, with a girl who was probably awake at first, a victim who's one seat away from him. Each time, Gregory is able to do a little more."

Ivy shivered.

"Gregory could try this on any victim," Lacey continued,

"but he's practicing on people you know, Ivy, enjoying his ability to make you squirm. I'm betting Kelsey's next."

"Just like before, picking off my friends one by one."

Lacey nodded. "Isolating you, scaring you—he's pretty good at it."

"What about Beth and Will?"

"They may be too strong for him now. Even if he is able to seed a dream in them, they will remain loyal and fight to the death for you."

"I don't want them to fight to the death!" Ivy cried. "My friends have been through enough."

"We can stop him," Tristan said. "When I had angel powers, I could travel in people's dreams."

Lacey shook her head. "This is different. Gregory didn't slip inside dreams that Max and Dhanya were having on their own. He seeded false images in their minds. It's like he's projecting his own movies."

"Can you figure out the process? Can you teach me how to do it?"

"It's forbidden, Tristan—one of the Big Ten: *Thou shalt not bear false witness*. It doesn't matter if it's images or words: No lying allowed."

"But not all lies are evil," he argued. "A lie can protect others."

"I'm telling you, Tristan—"

"I'm telling *you*!" he interrupted Lacey. "When Gregory

178

was alive in his own body, he drugged Ivy, then dressed in clothes like mine, trying to get her to cross the track as a train was coming. Later he tied Philip's jacket to the train bridge, to make her think Philip was on the bridge and in danger. He was creating false images to lure Ivy. He's doing it again. Only this time the images are inside his victims' minds."

Lacey nodded solemnly and turned to Ivy. "He's rehearsing for his big show, whatever that may be."

Tristan paced. "I could stop him, if I had the same powers. You can figure it out, Lacey, and if you can't—"

"No!" Lacey tried to catch Tristan by the arm. He freed himself easily from her materialized fingers. "Don't try it, Tristan."

He stopped and turned his head slightly, as if he heard something.

"What is it?" Ivy asked, glancing toward the patio doors, then over her shoulder toward the front hall.

Tristan looked away. "Nothing."

"Tristan?"

He wouldn't meet Ivy's eyes.

At last she said to Lacey, "I'll keep watch over Kelsey."

Lacey nodded. "Kelsey's next, but keep in mind, Ivy: These are just walk-throughs with bit-part actors. You're going to be the star of Gregory's little horror flick."

———

179

WHEN IVY RETURNED FROM TRISTAN'S, SHE FOUND Beth at Will's place, the two of them working on Corinne's flash drive. She quickly filled them in on Gregory's ability to seed dreams.

"I'm glad Suzanne's on the other side of the ocean," Beth said as she and Ivy walked back to the cottage. "Who knows what Gregory might have done to her!"

Ivy had been thinking the same thing. "Have you heard from her in the last week?"

"A text here and there. I've been sending her poems."

"You've been writing a lot." Ivy linked her arm through Beth's. "How come you haven't sent *me* any?"

"I—uh—just didn't think to. I'll . . . send you one."

"One?"

"Two."

"I want three!" She had been teasing Beth, but now as they passed in front of the lighted windows of the cottage, she saw that Beth was blushing. "I'm kidding you."

"I know you are. And I—I've always shown you everything." Beth drifted into silence.

Ivy wondered why Beth would suddenly feel reluctant. Was the poetry about Will? Maybe Beth thought that because Will and Ivy were once a couple . . . "Are they love poems?" she asked, following Beth into the cottage.

"Sort of. I mean, yeah." Beth laughed self-consciously. "That's the kind of stuff I write—nature and love poems."

Dusty had trotted in behind them, and he leaped up on Ivy's lap. Beth sat on the sofa next to her. "Ivy, do you ever think about September?"

"Yeah, I do." Ivy buried her fingers in the thick ruff around the cat's neck. "It's strange, isn't it? So many things are going to be different than we had thought when we got our college acceptance letters."

"I can't imagine being that far away from you. Trinity is two and a half hours from Manhattan!"

"It's going to be hard," Ivy acknowledged. "But you'll be just a subway ride from Will. I'm really glad you and he will be in the same city," Ivy added, trying to let Beth know she was happy for her and Will. "It can be a very romantic city."

Beth bit her lip and was quiet for a moment. "I don't want to lose our friendship, Ivy!" she blurted out. "Do you understand? You're too important to me. I don't want to do anything to risk our friendship."

Ivy stopped petting Dusty. "Beth, you and I've been to hell and back together. We're not going to lose our friendship."

"Not even if—" She hesitated.

"If . . . ," Ivy repeated, then finished the question for her friend, "you and Will have fallen in love?"

Beth nodded almost imperceptibly. Her eyes were wide and blue, making Ivy think of the endless possibilities glimpsed in a sky. There was an openness in her friend's face, not naïveté or innocence, but wonder. It was one of the traits that Ivy loved the most about her.

"I would be so happy if you have."

"Not that I have any reason to believe he—"

"Oh, I don't know about that!" Ivy said.

"But, Ivy, sometimes—more and more—he won't even look at me. Especially when we're sitting close. And he doesn't touch me, not the way he used to."

Ivy laughed. "You mean that old slap on the back like you're army buds?"

Beth made a face.

"So ask him why. He's changed the way he looks at you and touches you. There must be a reason why."

"Maybe." Beth reached for Dusty, but the cat leaped down from the sofa, alerting them to the conversation outside. The screen door was pulled open, Dusty ran out, and Bryan, Kelsey, and Dhanya came in.

"Hey, roomies," Kelsey said. "I've come home before the clock strikes twelve and my coachman turns into a rat."

A rat would be an upgrade, Ivy thought, eyeing Gregory.

"You feeling okay?" Beth asked after Kelsey flopped in a chair.

"No. My head hurts and I'm kind of dizzy."

"Like you were at the party?" Ivy couldn't hide her concern.

Bryan squeezed in next to her on the sofa and laid his

arm across the back of it, letting his fingers rest on her shoulder. "What do you think it could be, Ivy?"

She forced her shoulders to relax. If Gregory was working on Kelsey's mind, trying to seed a dream, he wanted Ivy to know it and be afraid. "Haven't a clue," she told him.

"She's been like this for the last hour," Dhanya said. "We were playing miniature golf and she sat out the last round. When we stopped for ice cream, she almost fainted."

"Did not," Kelsey insisted. "I told you—you guys were boring me to death. I was falling asleep."

Could Gregory induce sleep? Ivy wondered. Was he learning to put someone in a hypnotic trance before seeding a dream?

"Strange, isn't it, Ivy?" Bryan baited her.

"Not really. Kelsey goes to bed late and gets up early. She needs more sleep."

"She's not the only one," Bryan said, moving his head close to Ivy's. "How's Luke?"

Ivy shrugged. "Haven't heard from him."

"She's lying," Kelsey said, and was rewarded by the quick turn of Bryan's head. "She's been sneaking out at night to see him. Right, Dhanya?"

Dhanya gave Ivy an apologetic look.

"Sometimes she's come back smelling like she's been on the water, but not always. That's what you said," Kelsey reminded Dhanya.

Gregory had already trailed her part of the way to Tristan, Ivy thought. With this little tidbit, he now knew the hideout was close to the harbor. Denial would simply affirm it.

"She's seeing somebody," Kelsey said.

"Hot girls usually do." Bryan ran a finger along the chain of the amethyst pendant.

Ivy wanted to shove him back, but she was determined not to respond in a dramatic way that might gratify him.

Beth rose to her feet. "Bryan, we've got to be at work at six-thirty tomorrow. So, you should probably be moving on."

"Excuse me," Kelsey said, "he's my boyfriend. I'll tell him when to go."

But Bryan stood up. "Beth's right. It's getting late." He pulled Kelsey to her feet, kissed her hard on the mouth, then headed toward the door, smiling to himself. At the last moment, he turned back. "Sweet dreams."

Fourteen

AS SOON AS BRYAN LEFT, BETH CLOSED AND LOCKED the main door, although it was a different kind of invasion he had just threatened them with. Dhanya went directly to bed.

"Kels, how're you feeling now?" Ivy asked, noticing that her roommate was walking a little unsteadily toward the kitchen. "How about some soda and munchies?"

"I wouldn't mind," Kelsey replied, sitting down on the nearest chair. Beth, who was locking the back door, looked curiously at Ivy as she poured a sugary, caffeinated Coke over ice cubes. Then Beth nodded to signal her understanding, opened a kitchen drawer, and got out a pack of cards. Gregory seeded dreams when people were *asleep.* He had not succeeded when Kelsey was awake, but she was still under his influence. If they could keep Kelsey awake long enough to let the effect wear off . . .

Beth dealt, and Ivy poured two more sodas. "Cheers!" she said wryly, handing the Coke to Beth.

"Why don't we play for pennies," Beth suggested.

"Good idea," Ivy replied. Anything to goad Kelsey's competitive instinct and keep her awake.

An hour later, on her third Coke and still needing caffeine, Ivy asked, "Feeling better, Kels?"

Her roommate glanced down at the pile of coins she was amassing and grinned. "Much!"

Beth had fallen asleep. "Just let her be," Ivy said as she and Kelsey played on.

Forty-five minutes later, Ivy got up to stretch. With her back turned to Kelsey, she tried to peer through the window over the sink, but she couldn't see beyond the screen to the woods. How close did Gregory have to be to seed a dream? They couldn't stay awake all night.

"Want another Coke?" Ivy asked, pouring herself one.

When she didn't get an answer, she turned around. Kelsey's eyes were shut. Ivy hurried over to the table. "Kelsey, wake up."

Kelsey's back rested against the wooden chair, but her shoulders were slumped and her head had fallen forward. Ivy gently raised her chin. Beneath Kelsey's closed lids, her eyes moved rapidly—she was dreaming.

"Kelsey, wake up!" Ivy said sharply. She shook her by the shoulders, but Kelsey remained asleep.

"Beth," Ivy said, reaching for her friend's hand.

"What—what is it?" Beth asked, startled, then quickly awakened. Realizing what had happened, she rose from her chair. "Come on, Kelsey. Open your eyes!"

Kelsey was murmuring and twitching. Though her words and movements were hindered by sleep, she sounded angry. Sweat beaded her brow.

With light fingers, Beth slapped her on the cheek, then Ivy fetched ice cubes and rubbed them on Kelsey's hands and forehead.

Kelsey's eyes flew open. "Get away from me!" she cried.

Ivy stepped back. "I was just trying to—"

"I said *get away!*" Her eyes flashed and color burned high in her cheeks.

"Kelsey, hush," Beth said firmly. "Wake up. Clear your head. It was just a dream."

But Kelsey was furious. "You won't stop, will you, Ivy? I get it now. You always want the guy you can't have, the guy who's not yours. Luke, Bryan—you're hot for the challenge."

Ivy shook her head and laid a hand on Kelsey's arm. "Listen to me—"

Kelsey shook it off. "You compete for guys! That's your kind of sport!"

"Kelsey, calm down," Ivy said. "Tell me what you dreamed."

"It's not Luke you're sneaking out to see," Kelsey replied. "It's Bryan."

Ivy grimaced. Gregory had always been skilled at using a person's fears.

"You're fooling around with Bryan. I saw it with my own eyes."

"In your dream," Ivy said.

"Not just in my dream. I always see you guys together."

"But *Bryan* is the flirt. He does it just to push your buttons."

Kelsey struggled to get out of the chair. Her legs were wobbly. "Get away from me!"

"Not until we straighten this out."

"Get away!" Kelsey's voice became shrill. "I don't want you anywhere near me. Or Bryan!" She pushed past Ivy. Using the banister, she pulled herself up the steps to the bedroom.

Ivy felt Beth's hands on her arms, holding her in place. "She can't think past her dream," Beth said quietly. "Let it go."

"I'm not letting him win," Ivy argued back.

"If you force her to defend her dream, it will only make it more real in her mind. We'll try to reason through things tomorrow."

Ivy took a deep breath and let it out slowly. She doubted things would look any different to Kelsey in the morning. "It's just like before, Beth. He's going after the people close to me. No one's safe."

"It's you I'm worried about," Beth replied. "I can help Chase—at least, he's responding to my texts and phone calls. As for Kelsey, Dhanya, and Max—their dreams will fade. Gregory's just using them for practice." Beth reached for Ivy's fingers and placed her paler, dovelike hands around them, folding them as if in prayer. "You know who Gregory really wants to take down."

"Yes."

Beth rested her forehead against Ivy's. "I won't let him have you. Not ever!"

HIDDEN IN THE WOODS ABOUT SIXTY FEET FROM THE cottage, Tristan had been keeping silent guard. The woods behind him ran west and north, thinning along the tumbled stone wall that was the border between Aunt Cindy's and her neighbor's. When Tristan had arrived, the cottage's kitchen light was on, and it had stayed lit for a long time. He watched and waited, wondering how close Gregory had to be to seed a dream. His gut had told him Gregory would strike again quickly.

Suddenly, there was activity in the kitchen. Tristan heard Kelsey's raised voice. He wanted to charge the cottage, but he forced himself to remain hidden, suspecting that his quarry was doing the same. Thirty feet behind him, a dark shape slowly rose from the ground shadows and became a silhouette against the lighter mosaic of trees. Gregory lifted his arms and raised his face to the sky in triumph.

Anger burned in Tristan. A dark breeze, a flicker of malice, tossed the tree branches around them.

Gregory turned his head quickly, as if listening. "Hello, Tristan."

Tristan straightened up and walked toward him. "Gregory."

"You came for the show. I'm flattered."

"Don't be."

They met in a pool of moonlight at the base of a dead tree.

"Why are you viewing the show from back here?" Gregory asked in a genial voice. "Move closer. Peek in a window. Kelsey can be very entertaining."

"I'm not interested in Kelsey."

"You're interested in *anyone* who touches Ivy," Gregory replied, leaning against the charred tree. "And so am I."

A low, satisfied murmuring riffled the leaves around them.

With his index finger, Gregory traced the long scar of a lightning strike burnt in the tree's white flesh. "Power," he said, his voice as silky as a lover's. "Can you produce lightning, Tristan? Can you do it on demand?"

"I don't wish to."

Gregory laughed. "I didn't ask you what you *wish*." He tilted his head and looked Tristan up and down, as if assessing his strength. The body was Bryan's, but the arrogant pose was Gregory's. "I can't control lightning," he confessed, "not yet, but I can produce it. I've killed with it."

Tristan's hands itched to grab him by the throat and throw him to the ground. An ominous soughing stirred the trees.

"We're stuck in these bodies, aren't we," Gregory said. "The voices forgot to mention that little detail until I was securely inside this one. If we die in these bodies, we can't return."

"So maybe you should think twice before playing with lightning."

"Is that why you held back?" Gregory asked.

"What do you mean?"

"You knew my identity before I knew yours. Why didn't you strike first? What are you afraid of, Tristan?"

"Nothing."

Gregory snickered. "Anyone who has something to lose is afraid. That's the problem with love. It gives you something to lose."

The sinister murmur awakened into distinct voices: *Now. Ever. Ours.*

"Why aren't you dream seeding?" Gregory persisted. "It's a lot of fun."

"I don't need victims to make me feel like I'm alive."

"Back when I *was* alive," Gregory said, "you could slip inside people's minds. Mine, Eric's—you prowled around our dreams. This dream seeding ought to be a piece of cake for you."

The muscles in Tristan's arms tightened. His fists were sharp knuckles.

"Wait a minute," Gregory said, his voice charged with amusement. "I should have guessed it—you didn't *choose* to be in the body of a wanted murderer. You got your wings clipped!"

Now. Ever. Ours.

"What are you doing time for?" Gregory taunted. "Something to do with Ivy. She'll bring you down if anybody will."

Tristan struggled to control the emotions roiling within him.

Which way? Which way? the voices asked.

"What do you want, Gregory?"

"I think you know," the demon replied coolly.

"Revenge. But then, why are *you* holding back? You know where Ivy is, where I am. And you have nothing to lose. Why haven't you killed us?"

The power is within you, the voices said.

Gregory laid a patronizing hand on Tristan's shoulder. "The tragedy is, once Ivy's dead, the fun is over."

Tristan shook off his hand.

"Think about it, Tristan. It's the dying that's so entertaining."

A mix of anger and horror ran through Tristan's veins.

"I've watched Ivy have a great life at my expense—"

"At your expense!" Tristan exclaimed.

"And I deserve more," Gregory went on, "than watching her die a quick and painless death. *Bang bang, Ivy's dead*—how unsatisfying!"

You deserve more, the voices said.

"If you touch her," Tristan threatened, "if you do anything to hurt her—"

"She owes me! And I will make her pay." Gregory's words thrummed low and intense beneath the rising pitch of the voices. "I will draw her blood, drop by drop."

Tristan lunged at him. The voices shrilled with pleasure. He dragged Gregory to the ground, then pulled up and slammed his fist into Gregory's jaw again and again, until his knuckles bled.

The power is within you, the voices shouted.

Pinned beneath Tristan, Gregory fought back, his strong arms raising Tristan off his chest so he could roll out from under him. Leaping to his feet, Gregory kicked Tristan in the head, then hard in the gut, making him gasp for breath.

The power and the glory! the voices cried.

Struggling to stand, Tristan reeled backward into the dead tree. Gregory took off running for the old stone wall. Tristan raced after him, catching him at the base. Gregory scrambled up the pile of rocks. Tristan followed, grabbing him from behind. They struggled, and the loose stones at the top gave way. Grappling with each other, they slid together down the heap.

At the bottom, Tristan's fingers closed around the end of a jagged rock. It was too heavy to pick up in one hand. But as the voices grew in number, as their pitch climbed, a sudden, unnatural strength surged inside him. Kneeling on Gregory, grasping the rock, Tristan lifted his arm. The face below him stared up in terror. Tristan had Gregory where he wanted him: He would crush the serpent's head until Gregory's spirit bled out of it.

Take what is yours! the voices told him.

Gregory's life—and his own—this was what the voices wanted. If he killed, if he served hell's demons, he would be beyond redemption. But damnation was worth it, if it kept Ivy safe.

A sacrifice! A sacrifice! the voices screamed, triumphant. *Now, ever, ours!*

Now, ever . . . theirs. Theirs in hell for eternity, an eternity without Ivy. Forever without Ivy.

Tristan bowed his head. He was able to pray just two words. *Angels. Help.*

Slowly his grasp on the rock loosened, and the weapon slipped to the ground.

Standing up, Tristan dragged Gregory to his feet. "Get out of here!" He pushed Gregory away, though his hands still ached to hurt him. "Get out of my sight!"

Gregory rubbed his bruises, smirked at Tristan, then slunk away.

Fifteen

SUNDAY MORNING, WITH KELSEY STILL FUMING, IVY
and Beth switched jobs, Ivy teaming up with Will to serve
breakfast. While they were sweeping the last pastry crumbs
and flower petals off the porch, Beth joined them.

Will's face lit up. "Hey, ready for our bike ride this afternoon?"

Beth hesitated. "I was wondering if we could go in the
evening instead."

Ivy saw the disappointment on Will's face, though he
quickly hid it. "Did something come up?"

"During my break I talked to Chase."

"Oh."

When Will didn't say anything else, Ivy asked, "How is he?"

"He says he's okay," Beth replied, "but I can tell from his voice that he isn't. Will, I really think I should go over there this afternoon."

Will picked up a chair and returned it to its place near the end of the porch.

"I think Chase needs someone to talk to right now."

"You mean someone to listen to him," Will countered. "That's all he wants, an audience while he holds forth in all his brilliance."

"I can help him," Beth persisted.

Will raised an eyebrow. "You know a cure for an ego on steroids?"

Ivy smiled at the apt description.

"I've been through the same thing he has," Beth explained. "I'm the only other person who knows what it's like."

"So, he's admitting he was possessed," Will said.

Beth shook her head. "Well, no, not exactly."

"Didn't think so."

"Can't we ride later? It'll be cooler and prettier."

"Sure," Will replied. "Whenever." Turning his back, he moved another chair, one that didn't need to be repositioned.

Beth glanced up at Ivy, shrugged, then left. It was so tempting to assure Will he had nothing to worry about. Ivy felt as if she was bursting with the secret that each of them was keeping, but they needed to tell each other what was in their hearts, not have a friend fix things for them.

After work Ivy changed into cooler shorts and a hoodie, slipped her cell phone in her pocket, and headed toward the beach. When she reached the top of the long flight of steps to the dunes, she saw Will sitting on the landing halfway down. Ivy hesitated, then walked down slowly—noisily—giving him warning and trying to assess whether he wanted her company.

"Hey."

"Hey," he replied softly.

Ivy gazed out at the sea, following with her eyes its sweep around the end of Nauset Beach.

"So, did you tell Tristan about Kelsey?" he asked.

"I'm going to," she said, patting the phone in her pocket.

Sitting on the steps above the landing, Ivy leaned back against the boards, watching the gulls perform their aerial act above the frothy net of the ocean. Will's hands often betrayed his impatience with others, but they were still now. There was a chance he wanted to talk.

"Why does she still care?" Will blurted out.

"You mean why does Beth care about Chase?"

"It's not like he's been nice to her."

Ivy shrugged. "Beth is kind to people whether or not they've been nice to her. You know that. It's one of the reasons you and I love her."

"It's a girl thing," Will said, his anger surfacing. "Girls like needy guys."

"Whoa! Ex*cuse* me!" Ivy exclaimed, then laughed.

Will looked a bit sheepish. "Okay. But you have to admit, Beth has always been attracted to him."

Now we're getting somewhere, Ivy thought.

"You remember how she was the night we met him at the ice-cream shop," Will said. "She kept saying how 'gorgeous' he was, like he was the only guy who had ever grown a few inches taller, the only guy with a pair of shoulders. She said he was like one of her romance characters come to life."

Ivy thought back to that moment, when she and Will were still a couple. Perhaps what she had interpreted as grouchiness on Will's part was something more than either she or Will had realized at the time. Ivy began to smile.

"What?" Will asked, turning to look at her.

"I was just remembering how awful you were, when Chase was bragging about his skiing and you made up that story about your terrible accident and how your doctor warned that you might never walk again. For a moment poor Chase was speechless."

"It was a very short moment," Will replied, then laughed a little.

Leaning forward, he rested his elbows on his knees, his face serious again. Ivy studied Will's profile, his dark hair and dark lashes. She knew the depth in his soulful eyes.

"Will, everybody has a romantic dream of a lover, but when we meet the real one, and we feel love beyond anything we could ever imagine, that old dream person melts away."

She saw him swallow hard.

"Do you love her?" she asked.

"I care about her deeply."

"Good," Ivy said, "but that's not what I asked. Are you in love with Beth?"

He didn't reply. She followed his eyes and watched two boats slip through the inlet, venturing out of the protected waters, looking small against the expanse of ocean.

"Why don't you tell Beth how you feel?"

"I'll think about it."

"You're already in love—you can't undo those feelings. What do you have to lose by telling her?"

"My best friend."

"Because if her feelings aren't the same, you think she'll back away from you?"

He nodded.

"And yet, after all the grief that Chase has given her, obsessing over her and trying to control her, then running after Dhanya, she still cares enough to try to help him. Don't underestimate Beth's strength. When it comes to relation-ships, Beth is the strongest person I've ever known."

Will took a ragged breath. "I love her so much, I ache."

Ivy looked to her left, to where the working and pleasure boats would return to moor for the night and the water that lapped the shore where Tristan was hiding. "Yeah. Tell me about it."

AFTER A BEACH NAP AND WALK, IVY HEADED TO St. Peter's to practice piano, stopping for a takeout dinner on the way. Arriving at the church, she found the rectory closed up and a note taped to the door: *Fr. John will return at 6:30.* She decided to wait for the key and wandered around the building, to the priest's garden.

Ivy had visited it the day she brought along "Guy," as she had first called Tristan when she knew him simply as a hospital runaway. He had helped Father John dig a new bed for roses along the edge of his fenced-in vegetable patch. Now, inside the fence, tomatoes reddened on their leafy stems; purple eggplants hung from staked bushes like oversize Christmas ornaments; cucumbers and squash sprawled with their sunny flowers and waxy fruit. Against the white pickets the rose bushes, though still small, bore blooms that glowed with the colors of sunset. A folding chair had been placed next to them, and Ivy sat there to eat.

In the peace of the early evening, she forced aside her thoughts of Gregory and reviewed her list of piano assignments. Pulling out a book, she studied her newest piece of music, but she was unable to process the notes she read—she couldn't hear them in her head or hum them aloud. Despite her afternoon nap, she felt exceptionally drowsy. The colors of the summer evening faded.

A May storm was brewing. Ivy was driving, and the first raindrops pelted her windshield as she searched for a certain street address. Lightning flashed and the storm broke. She left her car and ran up a flight of steps toward a house with a picture window. She tried to peer through it, but all she could see were the reflections of the clouds and thrashing trees.

A feeling of dread grew in the pit of Ivy's stomach. She had done this before and knew that something in the house had the power to kill her. She turned away, but the need to see who or what was there drew her back. Peering through the window again, she saw a tall stone statue, an angel with an upraised arm and hand pointing to heaven. It tipped toward her. Glass exploded in Ivy's face.

She screamed and screamed.

"Ivy! Ivy, wake up!"

She opened her eyes and saw the kind face of Father John peering down at her. Keys and a ball of green twine lay on the grass next to him. The breeze felt warm and dry against her cheek, soft with the ginger and citrus smells of his roses.

"You were dreaming," the priest said.

Ivy took a deep breath and let it out slowly.

"A bad dream," he added sympathetically.

She nodded and glanced about. "Did—did you see any-one here?"

"In my garden?" The priest sounded surprised.

"Or the parking lot?"

He shook his head, frowning. "No."

It was her old nightmare, Ivy thought, but with a new twist. Last year it was the deer that crashed through glass, then the train. *Why an angel?* she wondered. The statue, while familiar, didn't look like any that Ivy had owned.

"In your church," Ivy said, "are there any depictions of angels with an arm raised and hand pointing upward?"

Father John looked at her curiously. "No. But that is a stance commonly found in cemetery statues."

Ivy shut her eyes for a moment. Gregory had finally succeeded in breaking into her mind, she thought, seeding the old dream and adding an ominous detail to scare her.

"Is everything all right?" the priest asked, sounding concerned. "Ivy, are you in some kind of trouble? Is some-thing or someone frightening you?"

"No. No, it was just a dream."

He looked at her closely, the small vertical line in his

brow deepening, then said, "You've come to practice piano. But sit here and finish your sandwich while I do a little work. I like the company."

She knew what Father John was doing—making sure she was all right, giving her time to talk if she wanted. She nibbled on her sandwich and watched as he carefully tied up his bounty of fruit and flowers.

"This is my favorite time of day in the garden," he told her. "You know what they say: One's nearer to God's heart in a garden than anywhere else on earth."

Ivy did her best to smile and nod. No garden, no corner of the earth, she thought, was safe from a serpent like Gregory.

Sixteen

PLAYING THE PIANO DID LITTLE TO CALM IVY THAT night. She left the church at eight fifteen and drove directly to Tristan's. Standing outside the Steadmans' house, she whistled a song from *Carousel*.

Tristan opened the door, then opened his arms. Ivy rushed into them. Leaving the door ajar, he held her tightly.

"Tristan."

He kissed her, then laid her head against his shoulder, pressing his cheek against hers, as if he guessed she wanted comforting most of all.

When he released her, Ivy touched his forehead. "Hey! What happened to you?"

Tristan rubbed his temple ruefully, and she saw a cut on his knuckles.

"I ran into an unfriendly piece of furniture. You'd think I'd know my way around this house by now."

"Does it hurt?"

"Only my pride," he replied lightly. "Let's go for a walk, okay?"

"It's still early. A lot of people are out," she said.

He took her hands in his. "Ivy, I feel less than human, creeping around like some nocturnal animal in the middle of the night. I need to be outside. I need to do the things normal people do."

Wrapping her arms around him, Ivy could feel the tension in his muscles. "Okay."

They walked the roads over to Town Cove, Ivy's hand in Tristan's, then returned to the narrow beach at the Steadmans' house, where they sat. The night air was cool, but the sand held some of the day's heat. Ivy burrowed her bare feet in the warm grains and leaned against Tristan. A single bird sang against the encroaching darkness.

"When you got here tonight, something was worrying you," Tristan said.

She combed the sand with her fingers. "I feel better now."

"Ivy. Tell me."

"Promise me you won't"—she hesitated—"overreact." She felt Tristan shift his position and knew that he didn't like her saying that. When she recounted her dream, he didn't speak, but he gripped her hand so hard she had to rub the backs of his fingers to get him to loosen them.

"Stay with me tonight, Ivy! Stay with me every night from now on."

"I can't do that, Tristan, not without attracting attention. Where would I say I'm staying?"

"It doesn't matter anymore! Ivy, he's closing in on"—he caught himself—"on us."

On you. She knew that's what Tristan had meant to say.

He held Ivy so tightly she could feel his heart pounding against her own ribs.

"With each dream that he seeds, his power is growing," Tristan said. "If he can do it from ninety feet away, then soon—"

Ivy pulled back slightly, puzzled. "Ninety feet? What makes you say that?"

Tristan was silent for a moment. "I saw him."

"Tonight?"

"Last night. In the woods outside the cottage."

"You were there? Tristan!"

"I couldn't just hide away and do nothing!"

Ivy shut her eyes. How far would Tristan go to stop Gregory? "Did he see you?"

Tristan didn't answer.

Ivy touched his bruised temple, then reached for his hand with the battered knuckles. "Tristan, please . . . please!" she begged. "Don't go near him again. Don't touch him. Promise me!"

Tristan looked away.

With gentle fingers she turned his face back to her. "I want the same thing as you do, love. To be together. But you can't destroy Gregory without destroying yourself."

"So I should just let him hurt you? Kill you?!"

"There's some other way," Ivy said. "There must be."

Tristan shook his head, then pulled her close and buried his face in her hair.

When Ivy's cell phone rang, neither of them moved. It stopped, then started again. Finally, Tristan let her go.

"It's Will's ringtone," Ivy said, slipping her phone from her pocket. "Hey there."

"Ivy, where are you?" Will's excited voice was loud enough for Tristan to hear. "I have something to show you."

"To show—?" She realized what it was. "You've found something on the flash drive!"

"Hit the jackpot!"

"Can you bring your laptop here? I'm with Tristan."

"If you tell me where *here* is."

Fifteen minutes later Will called to say he had parked two roads away. They left the front door ajar for him. When he stepped inside, he stopped, appearing uncomfortable, then shifted his laptop to his left hand. "Tristan." He held out his other hand. "I owe you an apology."

"I owe you more," Tristan replied, shaking his hand, "more than I can ever pay back."

Will turned to Ivy. "Wait till you see this! Where can I set up?"

They led him to the kitchen, and he opened his laptop on the island. With Ivy on one side and Tristan on the other, Will clicked on the directory tagged CORINNE and opened folders, then subfolders and files.

"Talk about finding a needle in a haystack!" Tristan remarked.

"Yeah," Will replied, "except there's a useful subset in here. Most of Corinne's files are JPEGs. You'd expect that from a photographer. But when you click on Details, you also see Photoshop files. The interesting thing about Photoshop files is that they contain layers of images. Let me show you."

He clicked on a photo of Corinne's grandmother sitting in her sewing alcove with her spools of thread and her button jar. On the right side of the computer screen was a box that listed layers with names like "filter 1," "filter 2," "glow," "shadow," "window pane," "wallpaper," and "jar."

Will pointed to the boxed list. "These layers come together to make the final picture. The artist can turn layers on and off to create different effects. But she can do more than that. She can order the layers so that some layers will hide others. And she can use color to mask things.

"See the letter *T* on this layer? It means the layer contains text, rather than an image. I found two Photoshop files with text in them, which seemed a little unusual. The text layer's off right now, but I'm going to turn it on." He clicked, and the symbol for a closed eye became open.

"I still don't see anything," said Tristan.

"Right. Because she adjusted the font color, and it's blending in. So, now I'm going to change the font color for our layer of text."

Ivy leaned forward. "I see letters. They look like hieroglyphics!"

"Hard to read," Will agreed. "So, let's change the color of the background layer, to create a better contrast, then turn all the other layers off, and simplify the font." Will made a few clicks.

Ivy gasped. A clear list appeared on the computer screen: Typed in columns were names, dates, and numbers—amounts of money, she guessed.

"Bryan S," Tristan read aloud, "June 10, July 10, September 12—looks like he missed August."

"What's 'Seneca Hall 436'?" Ivy asked, reading along with Tristan. The words were typed next to "September 12."

"A dorm room," Will replied. "I googled a campus map. Corinne must have lost track of Bryan when he first moved to college, but she caught up with him again."

"He's resisting her pressure," Tristan observed. "The pay dates get later and later. She doesn't get December's payment till New Year's Eve."

"And in March, the month before she dies, she doesn't get the full amount," Ivy noted.

Will pointed at the screen. "Look at the different amounts for the victims, not only different amounts but different schedules. From Tony M., she collected every other month."

"Tony Millwood," Ivy guessed. "I bet she was blackmailing the guy with the body shop."

"Corinne was sharp," Tristan said. "She figured out what she could get from her different victims without pushing them over the edge, guaranteeing herself a steady income. The only person she seemed to have misjudged was Bryan."

"Several hundred a month. Even when you're on scholarship, that's a lot," Ivy reasoned.

Tristan grimaced. "Especially for a guy who murders people when they become inconvenient."

"Since a photo of Corinne's grandmother masked the blackmail list, I searched for other photos of her, figuring they might hide something, which this one did." He clicked on it.

"The cufflink!" Ivy said happily.

"I've got something else to show you. Let me switch folders. Corinne did a fabulous shoot at a body shop—the one belonging to Tony?"

Ivy nodded.

"Well, her least interesting photo has a very interesting Photoshop file. The top two layers are photos of a dark sedan."

"Hank's," Ivy and Will said at the same time, recognizing the vehicle belonging to Corinne's stepfather.

"A completely different car is photographed in the layers beneath it, a car with front-end damage."

Ivy and Tristan exchanged glances. "Bryan's?"

Will kept clicking on layers. "She took the trouble to snap a clear photo of its license plate."

"'HATTRIK,'" Tristan read. "*Hat trick* is a term used in hockey."

"And this."

Ivy leaned forward, squinting at the long number.

"It's a VIN," Will told her. "Vehicle identification number. Each car has its own, engraved when the car's built."

"So even if you claimed stolen tags, it would be proof of the car's ownership," Tristan said.

To Ivy it felt as if a mountain had been lifted off her shoulders. Even in the dim light created by the laptop, she could see the difference in Tristan. He seemed to stand taller, the same burden lifted from him.

"You're going to be free, Tristan!" she said, hugging him, then Will. "Will, I'll need you to go with me to the police and show them what you've found. Once we've convinced them, I'll take them to the safe-deposit box where I have Corinne's note, flash drive, and the envelope they came in."

"If you can give me another twenty-four hours, I may be able to find more material—like photos that were used for blackmailing the others. You want to put enough pressure on the blackmail victims for them to come clean to the police, so you have a solid case that Corinne was blackmailing Bryan."

Ivy and Tristan agreed. A few minutes later, they walked Will to the front door.

"I don't know how to thank you," Tristan said.

"If we keep thanking and apologizing to each other," Will replied, "we'll never get on to just being friends. Let's call it even and done."

Tristan smiled. "Even and done."

After Will left, Ivy turned to Tristan. "You know I can't stay here tonight."

"I know I can't make you do something you don't want to."

"Tristan! It's not that I don't want to. It's like what you said earlier: I can't just hide out here and do nothing.

Gregory's desire to hurt me has already hurt enough other people. I need to be at the cottage for Dhanya, Kelsey, and Beth."

He nodded.

"I'll come as soon as I finish work tomorrow," she promised.

"I want to go to the cemetery where Michael Steadman's buried."

Ivy looked at Tristan with surprise.

"I think a lot about him. His things are still in this house, his clothes, his trophies—swimming trophies like I had. I feel a connection with him. I want to see where he's buried and pay my respects." Tristan looked a little self-conscious. "I sound like my father, don't I?"

Ivy smiled. "You sound like the guy I'm in love with. We'll go there tomorrow." She held his face in her hands. "Tristan, we'll be together soon. Soon there will be nothing separating us."

He kissed her and let her go very slowly, as if, in releasing Ivy, every centimeter that he opened his arms and spread his fingers made him ache.

"Love you, Tristan."

"Love you, Ivy."

She slipped out the front door and through the shadows of the yard, making her way silently to her car. Fifteen minutes later, when she pulled into the inn's parking lot,

Chase's car was pulling out. Beth waited for her.

"How's it going?" Ivy greeted her friend.

"Okay."

"Did you stay for dinner?" Ivy asked, remembering that Beth was supposed to have returned for an evening bike ride with Will.

"I called Will. Twice." Beth sounded hurt. "He didn't answer."

"He was pretty involved with something," Ivy replied, but she wanted Will to be the one to tell Beth what he'd discovered. They found him sitting in one of the Adirondack chairs, staring at the garden, lost in thought. Hearing their footsteps on the grass, he looked up.

"Hey." His slight smile was for Ivy, not Beth.

"I tried to call you, Will."

"Yeah, I saw."

Ivy looked from one to the other, then sat on the swing and pulled Beth down with her.

"So, how was Chase?" Will asked.

"Okay. He didn't want to listen to me, but he didn't want me to leave, either. You know Chase."

"I know Chase," Will replied dryly.

Beth pushed the swing back and forth with one foot. "I think I can help him."

"I'm sure you can." The moment Beth looked away, Will grimaced.

"I just have to be patient."

"You've always been good that way," Will said. "So, I guess you'll be spending a lot of time with him . . . ?"

Beth shrugged. "Whatever he needs."

"That's really nice," Will told her. "You're the nicest friend a guy could have, Beth."

Beth stiffened. Ivy guessed it wasn't what she wanted to hear from him. Poor Will, attempting to be the perfect, understanding male friend—he should have memorized one of the impassioned lines from Beth's stories and tried that instead.

"If you don't watch out, Beth," Will said, "Chase will fall in love with you." As soon as he'd spoken, he looked as if he wished he hadn't.

Beth stared at him.

Will backpedaled quickly. "Unless of course you want Chase to. I'm not saying there's anything wrong with you and Chase falling in love."

Beth blinked.

"In fact, *visually*—you know, if I was looking for a pair of models—I'd have to say you'd make a really great couple."

Hoo-boy! thought Ivy.

Beth frowned. "Just shut up, Will!"

Close to tears, she walked quickly through the garden and around the side of the inn.

"What'd I say wrong?" Will asked, throwing up his hands. "I don't get it! It's like all of a sudden I can't talk to her right. It was the model part, wasn't it," he guessed. "I thought I was being supportive."

"Sometimes you can support the wrong cause."

"Ivy, I can't be her friend and watch her fall in love with him. He could be the greatest guy in the world, and I still couldn't!"

"Did it ever occur to you that's what she's hoping to hear?"

A long and thoughtful silence followed, then Ivy's phone sounded at the same time as Will's.

"It's Suzanne," Ivy said. "A text."

WHO JUST BROKE BETH'S HEART?

WHY WON'T SHE SAY WHO THIS MYSTERY GUY IS?

SHE'S SENT ENOUGH LOVE POEMS

TO WALLPAPER MY ROOM.

Ivy peeked up at Will to see if he was reading the message. "Does yours begin 'Who just broke Beth's heart'?"

"Yes." He studied the text as if he was translating it. Amazement lit his face.

"So," said Ivy, "shall I tell Suzanne that you'll get back to her after you've talked to Beth?"

He looked at Ivy with a smile that would melt all the stars in the Northern Hemisphere. "Yeah, you tell her that." He turned toward the inn.

"I'd try the stairway to the beach," Ivy advised, and laughed when he set off at a run.

Seventeen

WILL AND BETH, IVY THOUGHT HAPPILY AS SHE AND Tristan walked together late Monday afternoon. Sometimes love started with bewildering passion and then grew deeper through friendship; sometimes it started with deep friendship and surprised everybody—especially the two "best friends"—with its sudden romantic fire. Either way, love seemed both meant to be and a miracle.

Ivy glanced behind her. Tristan was crouching down, reading an epitaph on an old stone. The day was unusually hot for the Cape, and they had decided to visit Michael

Steadman's grave before the evening thunderstorms rolled in. It was a chance worth taking, Tristan being out in the open. Tomorrow, she and Will had an appointment with Rosemary Donovan, the officer most familiar with the case, a meeting to which they would bring their evidence. Soon Tristan would be able to walk anywhere.

Ivy glanced up at the sky. The clouds had gathered earlier than predicted. The glossy white of summer cumulus, rising with the heat, had become towering thunderheads, their underbellies darkening. With the sun masked, the grass faded and the trees turned a foreboding olive color, the undersides of their leaves twisting up in the breeze.

Ivy didn't remember there being so many trees when she had been there two weeks ago. She glanced over her shoulder to call to Tristan and discovered she had walked around a bend and could no longer see him. Despite the warmth of the day, a cold uneasiness settled in the pit of her stomach. Her arms, damp with sweat, got goose bumps. She could smell the approaching storm, but the smell was different from the salty humidity of the Cape; it was green— verdant—mossy.

Ivy turned slowly, surveying the leaning stones. The rain had cried away some of the names and sentiments, but the statues spoke through the silence: a stone dog guarding his master, a wistful-looking youth holding a wreath of flowers, a lamb asleep on a tiny grave. Perhaps it was the dream that Gregory had seeded that made her notice two angel statues she hadn't seen before.

The road climbed higher, then dipped down again. Ivy entered an area in which a family's name became important, blazoned on tall obelisks and the lintels of private mausoleums. The row of stone buildings was sunk into a hillside. Styled like miniature Greek temples, some had no windows; others had windows that had been broken or removed, and replaced with iron bars. She shivered at the thought of being left inside one of these dismal houses of bones.

The Baines family was buried across from such a row of tombs, along Ravine Way. She remembered the plot . . . then she saw it: graves with individual headstones laid out around a tall monument, the land rising behind it. She gasped, recognizing the statue. Fifteen feet above the ground an angel stood, her left hand resting on an anchor, her right arm raised and hand pointing upward. A large tree grew at the far corner of the plot. The old copper beech, perhaps fifty feet wide and nearly as tall, dominated the landscape, its heavy limbs shading a quadrant of the tombstones, its reddish leaves forever weeping onto the family's graves.

Ivy walked slowly toward the massive tree, stepping around the family graves, and stopped beneath its dark canopy. *Gregory Thomas Baines,* she read from the surface of his shiny stone. *At Peace.* It was Ivy's mother who had suggested the epitaph, who had made that vain wish.

Ivy gazed down at the soft swelling of earth where Gregory was supposed to be at rest, listening to the wind gathering in the trees. It moved from grove to grove in the cemetery, and yet the leaves of the beech tree hung lifeless. Then the leaves on the lowest limbs began to tremble, and the trembling moved from the lowest twigs upward. Ivy heard a groaning from beneath the earth. The ground at her feet broke open. Gregory, in his own body, rose up like a dark angel.

She screamed and stepped back. Gregory moved with her, matching her step for step. His gray eyes burned with hate so intense it singed and shriveled the skin of his face.

Ivy wanted to run, but was afraid to turn her back on him. "Tristan!" she called out. "Tristan, help me!"

The wind whipped around the copper beech, and still Gregory and she moved within the silent eye of the storm's fury. His clothes hung motionless on his emaciated body.

"Mine," he said, his voice like a moan from beneath the earth. "All mine."

She shrank from the anguish she saw in his eyes. He raised his arm and she felt a cold that burned. His fingers stretched and curled like talons. She stepped sideways, slipping away from him.

"Look what you've done to me," he said. He turned his head to the right. She saw the gash on the left side of his skull, tarred with blood. Then Gregory twisted the trunk of his body, and Ivy gasped. His shirt hung torn over a protruding bone, a piece of his spine, broken in his fall from the railroad bridge.

His face swung back to her. "Vengeance is mine!"

Ivy shook her head. "You did this to yourself."

He laughed, and the air smelled of damp earth and decaying leaves. "Better say your prayers. It's your turn, Ivy. It is written: Vengeance is mine!"

"'Saith the *Lord*,'" Ivy replied, finishing the quote from the Bible. "Vengeance is *His*, not ours."

Gregory lunged for her. Ivy tore free from his grasp and ran. She could hear a rasping sound behind her, like breathing torn by sharp bones. It was coming closer and closer.

"Angels, help me!"

Her toe caught on a stone curb. She tumbled forward. Her hands went out in front of her, but she couldn't catch herself. "Angels! Angels!"

"Ivy, no!"

Hands yanked her backward. Tires shrieked.

"My God, girl! Watch where you're going!" The man's voice was both angry and scared.

"Ivy, listen to me! Come back to me!" Tristan pleaded.

Ivy blinked and looked around her. Just a few trees

shaded the cemetery from the bright afternoon sun. The graves had simple headstones. Directly in front of her was a narrow cemetery road. Tristan held Ivy from behind, as if he'd pulled her back just before she'd tumbled into the path of a van. The driver glared at her, then drove on.

Ivy sank back against Tristan. Her heart was still racing, and her head hurt. "What happened?"

"I'm not sure." He led her to a bench, holding her firmly as they walked, then easing her onto it, keeping her close to him as he sat down.

She tried to get her bearings. "I'm on the Cape."

"Where did you think you were?" Tristan asked.

"Riverstone Rise." She heard his sharp intake of breath.

"The cemetery at Stone Hill," he said. "Where I'm buried."

"And where Gregory's buried." She shuddered. "It was so real, Tristan. He was there, looking as he did after he fell from the train bridge."

"And he was chasing you," Tristan guessed. "You were running, Ivy, your eyes wide open, but not seeing where you were going. You looked awake and terrified, but I couldn't get through to you. Then you tripped on a grave marker and almost fell in front of the van."

Ivy buried her face in his shoulder. "Hold me, just hold me."

He tightened his arms around her. Laying his cheek

224

against her head, he rocked her gently. "I'm here. You're safe."

Ivy tried to push the frightening images out of her mind. "Tristan, Gregory can do more than seed a dream. He can create a waking vision."

Tristan swallowed hard and turned his head to look toward the road.

She knew what he was thinking. "He doesn't need to track me down with a gun. If you hadn't been here just now, I would have—"

Tristan laid his finger on her lips. "Hush, my love. It's not going to happen. I won't let it."

She said no more, as if Tristan had put an end to her newest fears. But he couldn't quiet her mind and heart. *As long as no one else suffers*, Ivy told herself. *Angels, help me.*

TRISTAN WAS SCARED. HE HAD BEGGED IVY TO STAY at the house with him, but she'd insisted on returning to the cottage for a few hours, before rejoining him after dark. "I'm okay," she kept saying.

If she knew how she had looked at him during the dream vision: like he was the devil himself! Tristan shuddered at the memory. How could he defeat someone who could control a mind to the point that the victim saw only what Gregory willed?

Tristan vowed he would fight Gregory to the death, but

for the first time, he wasn't sure that would be enough to save Ivy and himself. He paced the house. Dinnertime came and went; he wasn't hungry. A brilliant sunset faded; he didn't care. He waited in the dark, unable to think of anything but Ivy and how to keep her safe.

Then he heard it, the light whistling of a song from *Carousel*. His relief and joy were so intense he almost laughed out loud. He hurried to the door and opened it.

A gloved hand grabbed Tristan by the arm and jabbed him with a needle. He looked up just in time to see Bryan's face and the moonlit night crumble into darkness.

"AHOY, MATEY. AHOY, MATEY." THE PARROTLIKE VOICE startled Ivy out of her thoughts. She had just emerged from the shower when Philip's phone call came through. She shook out her hair and glanced at the clock: ten-fifteen.

"Ahoy. Why aren't you in bed?"

"I am," her brother replied. "I'm under the sheets."

Ivy laughed.

"Mom said we would call you tomorrow."

"Call me . . . about?"

"My tree house. It was set on fire."

"What?!"

"It's gone. The firefighters had to chop it out of the tree with their axes."

"Someone set it on fire?" Ivy sat down on the bed.

"Last night."

Her mind raced ahead. She seethed with anger: If Gregory dared to try it again, dragging Philip into his battle with her — "Why didn't Andrew and Mom call me?"

"They said they would tomorrow, when they knew more. The fire investigator and police came today."

"What did they find?" Ivy asked, trying to keep her voice calm.

"That somebody dumped stuff on it to make it burn."

"You mean an accelerant of some kind?"

"Yeah. They think it was some teenagers around here. "

Ivy steadied herself. Vandalism happened.

"But it wasn't," Philip said.

"Why—what makes you say that?"

"I saw him."

She forced herself to be patient. "Saw?"

"Gregory."

Ivy shut her eyes and a sick feeling washed over her. Then she thought quickly: To contradict Philip, to lie and tell him it wasn't possible, would not reassure him. Her little brother had the same certainty in his voice as when he first told her he saw Angel Tristan.

"How do you know it was Gregory?" she asked.

"He was watching the fire, and he turned to look at me."

The skin on the back of Ivy's neck prickled.

"He looked up at my bedroom window and pointed at

me. His face was different, but it was Gregory."

"Philip, don't go near that person! No matter what he says or does, don't listen to or believe him. Don't let him in. Don't go out to him. Do you understand me?"

"Dad's setting the house alarm tonight."

Which meant "Bryan" couldn't break in undetected, but what about Gregory? What could he do from afar?

"And I have my angel statues."

Oh, Angels, protect him, Ivy prayed. Aloud she said, "I'm coming home. Call Lacey and ask her to stay with you until I get there."

"I'm not scared."

Ivy was pulling on her jeans as she spoke. "Just call Lacey. Do it for me, okay?"

She grabbed a clean T-shirt and her sneakers. In her haste she knocked things off the top of her bureau— earrings, her comb, and keys. A round piece of gold caught her eye. She picked up Philip's angel coin and slipped it into her pocket. *Angels, protect him.*

Five minutes later, she was in her car and flipping open her second phone to call Tristan. Then she set it down again. If she told him about this, he'd want to come with her. He'd vowed to fight Gregory to the end—until one of them died, she thought, and it couldn't be Tristan. She started the car and headed for the Mid-Cape Highway. Just after crossing the canal, she pulled over to the side of the road and called Will's and Beth's cell phones. Neither one answered. For a moment, Ivy smiled, thinking of them in their new world together, remembering what it had been like when she and Tristan first confessed to each other that they were in love.

Ivy texted the same message to both of them: WORRIED ABOUT PHILIP. GOING HOME. TAKE EVIDENCE TO POLICE ASAP. THANX. LOVE.

"Lacey," she called out as she pulled back onto the road. "Lacey, I told Philip to call you. I need you to watch over Philip. Please!" Hopefully, Lacey was already there. Ivy knew the angel was more likely to respond to Philip than herself.

Ivy was speeding down the dark stretch of Route 25 when she had to hit her brakes and veer to avoid a hitchhiker. What a stupid and dangerous place for a person to—she braked again and looked in her rearview mirror.

"Why am I not surprised?" Ivy muttered, pulling over to the shoulder, then backing up.

"I was wondering if you'd see me," Lacey said, climbing into the car.

"If I'd hit you, what would have happened?" Ivy asked.

"I don't know. My soul would continue on. I guess the rest of me would just go *poof!*"

"All the same, now that you're riding with me, buckle your seat belt."

"Now that I'm riding with you," Lacey scoffed. "You're the one who summoned me."

After the angel complied, Ivy continued down the highway. "I was hoping Philip would call you. I told him to."

"He called, but he was sound asleep when I got there. What's up?"

Ivy told Lacey about Philip's conviction that Gregory had set fire to the tree house, then recounted the waking vision she'd had of Gregory in the cemetery.

"He's way too powerful," Lacey said.

"I know. Would you go back to Philip and stay with him until I get there?"

Lacey remained silent for a moment. "I will. But I think you're the one who's most in danger."

"I can handle Gregory."

"Getting a little cocky, aren't you?"

Ivy shrugged.

"Where's Tristan?"

"At the Steadmans' house, I guess."

"You haven't called him?" Lacey asked. "You haven't told him what you're doing?"

"I will," Ivy replied. "I'm just waiting till I'm far enough from the Cape not to be tempted to go back and get him."

Lacey leaned forward, straining against her seat belt,

until Ivy felt her staring. The angel nodded in approval. "Sometimes, chick, you surprise me," she said, then disappeared. A half second later, as if it was an afterthought, Ivy heard an unnecessary sound effect. *Poof!*

Eighteen

TRISTAN AWOKE TO THE DISTANT RUMBLE OF THUN-
der. The stillness around him told him he was alone. His
hands were tied. A rope hung loosely around his legs.
Sitting up slowly, he tried to make sense of the chilly air, the
hard stone bed beneath him, and the pervasive scent of rot-
ting things—leaves and something more animal-like.

Pale moonlight sifted in through the round eye of a window, an aperture covered with a grate. About a foot too
high for him to see out of, the window was set in a gable
that supported the low roof of his prison. Slipping one

foot then the other out of the rope that had bound his legs, Tristan stood cautiously, not knowing what he might step on. His hands still tied together, he struggled to feel the wall across from him. There was a long straight edge, parallel to the ground, and then another like it several feet above it. Everything that his fingers touched was damp stone. Tristan shivered. His prison was a mausoleum.

He thought back to Ivy's waking dream. Had Gregory brought him to Stonehill's cemetery?

He awkwardly felt the pocket where he kept his cell phone: gone. Moving toward the window, he bumped into something knee-high, knocking it aside. It sounded like wood tumbling against stone. Bending over, feeling for the object, he found and set the crate in front of the window so he could step up and look outside.

The slice of moon was blotted by mist, but Tristan could make out the shapes of the grave markers across from the mausoleum, ghostly white, some of them standing straight, others leaning with weariness. His eyes shifted to an impressive monument, a tall base supporting an angel. He had been here before, at the funeral of Gregory's mother. He remembered the dark tree that spread its heavy limbs above one corner of the Baines plot, the corner where she—and he assumed Gregory— was buried.

Scanning the landscape, Tristan saw no one. He

decided against calling out; if Gregory was nearby, it would tell him that Tristan had regained consciousness. Stepping down from the box, using his fingers as much as his eyes, he explored the surface of the metal door beneath the window. Its center seam and double set of hinges indicated that it was two doors. Neither panel had a handle, meaning the doors were not intended to be opened from inside the mausoleum. Even so, he pressed against them. They gave slightly along the seam, and he suspected that they were secured by something added on the outside, like a padlock or bolt.

He rested against the door, thinking. Gregory had gone to a lot of trouble putting him here. Bryan's body was strong, but it couldn't have been easy to lug Tristan to a car, then drag him from the car to the mausoleum. The rope around Tristan's feet had been loosened—to let him walk part of the way? Tristan didn't remember being conscious enough to move. So why did Gregory untie his feet? And why did he give him a box to stand on?

The answer was simple: Gregory wanted to make it easy for Tristan to look out the window. He wanted Tristan to know where he was, or maybe he wanted him to see something that was about to happen.

Tristan began to shake. Gregory had hinted at his plan the last time they met.

I deserve more, Gregory had insisted, *than watching her*

die a quick and painless death. Gregory had primed Ivy's mind with the waking vision at the Baines family plot. It had been a kind of dress rehearsal; tonight was the performance. *Think about it, Tristan,* he had said. *It's the dying that's so entertaining.* Just as entertaining to Gregory's warped soul would be watching Tristan watch Ivy slowly and painfully die.

Tristan stood back, then hurled himself against the door, determined to break out. He tried again and again, smashing his shoulder into the door, then sank to his knees. "Lacey!" he cried out. "I need you. Ivy needs you. Lacey, where are you?"

HALFWAY UP THE LONG DRIVEWAY LEADING TO HER Stonehill home, Ivy tried Tristan's phone again. She was growing uneasy. It was nearly 3 a.m.—too long for Tristan to be out of touch. As soon as she saw Lacey, she'd ask her to check on him.

Running the rest of the way to the top of the ridge, Ivy skirted the large clapboard house and turned toward the stone wall that marked the edge of the property. When she saw the blackened maples, her heart fell. A short distance from the trees lay a pile of burnt wood, the broken skeleton of Philip's wonderful tree house.

The tree house had been Gregory's as a child. Hoping to win the love of his newest son, Andrew had rebuilt and expanded it for Philip, never guessing it would become one more thorn to prick Gregory's jealousy. Ivy recalled the day Philip, stepping on a loosened plank, nearly fell from the walkway. She could still see the glow of wonder on her brother's face when he told her his angel had saved him. A year later, one of Ivy's first clues that Tristan had returned to her was his description of a tree house identical to Philip's. Just a few weeks back she had slept there with Tristan beneath a canopy of leaves and stars. But for Gregory, every symbol of love, every sign that people cared about one another, diminished him and must therefore be destroyed.

Turning away from the scorched trees, Ivy ran across the lawn to the back door. After disabling the house's alarm system, she crept up the steps, entered her own room, then crossed through the joint bathroom to Philip's. She looked around but couldn't spot Lacey's glow. Philip stirred in his bed, rolling onto his side.

"Ivy?"

"Shhh! Yes," she said softly. "Where's Lacey?"

Her brother sat up, blinking his eyes for a moment, as if trying to remember. "She said she had to go."

"But I told her—" Ivy bit her tongue.

"She said you'd be mad," Philip added.

Ivy nodded and smiled a little.

"I'm supposed to tell you that Tristan kept calling to her

and she had to see what kind of mess he had gotten himself into."

"When was all this?" Ivy asked quickly.

Philip looked at his bedside clock uncertainly. "She came after I called you. She left before I fell asleep again."

Ivy sighed. "Did she come back after she saw Tristan?"

He shook his head.

"Did she mention where she was going?" Ivy asked hopefully.

"Somewhere close. I told Lacey where he lived on the Cape, but she said he was somewhere close by."

Close by . . . *The cemetery,* Ivy thought.

Gregory could have frightened her with a lot of different waking visions, but he had chosen the setting at Riverstone Rise to send a message to her, to tell her where he could be found. He had drawn her back to Connecticut, where it had all started, with the one action that he knew would make her come home: threatening Philip. Now he counted on her to recall her waking vision, dangling it like a fishing lure in her mind's eye, the moment she feared for Tristan.

If she went to the cemetery, she would be taking Gregory's bait. But how could she not go? Lacey hadn't returned, and Tristan wasn't responding to Ivy's call: Something was very wrong.

"I'll help you look for him," Philip said, pushing back his sheet.

She caught him. "No!"

He raised his chin to argue with her.

"Tomorrow, Philip. I want you to get some sleep now so you're ready to help tomorrow."

He set his jaw.

"It could be a long day," she added.

"Why?"

She laughed and sat down on the bed next to him. "Because tonight's already been a long night. Do you remember the prayer we used to say?"

He shook his head no, but he was tired and finally relented, nodding yes. Together they said, "Angel of light, angel above, take care of me tonight, take care of everyone I love."

"That's you, Ivy," Philip added, as he had when he was a little kid.

Ivy rested her forehead against his. "Turn over. I'll rub your back."

He snuggled down with his pillow, and his eyes quickly closed. Asleep, he looked like the little boy she had mothered years back, when Maggie had to work long hours at her job. Ivy smoothed his hair and ran her fingers along his cheek. For a moment she felt as if she couldn't bear to leave him.

But he would be all right. The weight of Gregory's hate seemed to have only one effect on her brother: to make him stronger. She tiptoed out of the room.

Downstairs, Ivy quietly reset the house alarm. The moment she stepped out the door, she felt the change in the weather. The wind was damp and coming from the west now, a storm brewing. Ivy ran to her car. She checked the cell phone that she used for Tristan. No calls. Checking her other phone, she saw Will and Beth had texted her: They had gone directly to the police station and were waiting for Rosemary Donovan to arrive. Ivy slipped Tristan's phone in her pocket, set the other one on the passenger seat, and headed for the cemetery.

By the time she reached the entrance to Riverstone Rise, the sky in the west was flickering with lightning. Ahead of her, illuminated by headlights, the tall iron gates appeared to be chained, but when she got out of the car and pulled on the steel links, she discovered one of them had been pried open. She hurriedly slipped off the chain. After driving through, she stopped and glanced in her rear-view mirror. The wide-open gates offered an invitation to anyone who noticed them to follow her, but she continued on.

She tried to remember the way to the Baines plot. "Lacey," she called out, "where are you? Where's Tristan?"

She turned right, passing the oldest graves, then followed the narrow road as it climbed higher. When she reached the crest of the hill, she heard the dark rumblings of the approaching storm. A vicious streak of lightning buried its root in the next ridge. Ivy rolled down her car window. The smell was familiar: green—verdant—mossy.

The road before her suddenly dipped. At the bottom she veered onto Ravine Way, stopping her car where the row of mausoleums began. She leaned forward in her seat, hoping for some sign of Tristan, but she couldn't see beyond the two misty paths her headlights made in the humid air. The rest of the landscape was lit only by flashes of lightning. For half seconds at a time, the statues in the cemetery came alive, then turned back into faceless actors on a darkened stage.

If Gregory was hiding, her car lights had already told him where she was, but they had revealed nothing useful to her. She cut them and the engine, then got out. Walking quickly, she felt the first splinters of rain on her face. She imagined the eyes of the dead peering out the barred windows of their stone houses. She shifted her gaze to her right. Although the grave plots opposite the mausoleums were flat, the land rose sharply behind them; she felt as if she was passing through a ghostly gap in the fabric of the living world.

The wind picked up, suddenly finding its way into the ravine. Ahead of her and to the far right she saw the dark mass of the beech tree that marked a corner of the Baines plot. A crooked wire of lightning seared the sky to the west, thunder cracked, and the rain came down.

"Tristan!" she called out. "Tristan, are you here? Lacey? Where are you?"

Ivy . . . Ivy.

She started running.

Ivy.

At the edge of the Baines plot, she tripped over a low stone and tumbled forward, tasting grass and mud. Pulling her knees under her, she quickly stood up. In a sharp flash of violet white, she saw him.

"Oh my God! Tristan!"

He stood at the top of the Baines monument, more than twelve feet off the ground. Another flash of lightning showed her the heavy ropes that bound him to the stone angel. Ivy stared up with amazement and fear, wondering how she could reach him. Why wasn't Lacey here?

"Ivy, hurry!" A double flash of lightning showed the anguish on Tristan's face. Something dark stained his shirt, oozing from his chest. He was bleeding. He was going to die.

Ivy reached in her pocket for her cell phone and hunched her shoulders, sheltering it from the rain. *911. 911. 911.* She pressed the buttons over and over, but nothing happened.

"Tristan, try to hold on!"

The sound of laughter spun her around. In vain she

looked for Gregory. There were too many hiding places, too many stones for him to crouch behind. She turned back to Tristan. "I'm coming! Hold on!"

If Tristan died, fallen from grace—

"IVY," TRISTAN CALLED, HIS VOICE HOARSE FROM shouting. He peered through the blowing rain, his fingers gripping the window grate of the mausoleum. Lacey had been able to untie his hands, but she didn't have the physical strength to break the padlock that Gregory had placed on the door's hasp.

"I tried to stop her," Lacey said. "I tried to keep her from getting out of the car. I ran down the road right next to her, fully materialized—"

"I saw you."

"But she didn't!"

"She was already in his power," Tristan said, watching Ivy as she stood at the base of the monument, staring upward yet seeming oblivious to the dangerous lightning. Her mouth moved, but the storm drowned out her voice.

"What is it?" Tristan asked, his soul filled with dread. "What is she seeing?"

"You," Lacey said softly. "I'm just guessing—I can't see the waking vision any more than you can. But who else would hold Ivy's attention like that?"

"I've got to stop him! He's going to kill her!"

"Stop him, but don't kill him. Remember, Tristan—"

A sharp streak of lightning caught Tristan's eye. He heard the strike, felt the crack of thunder shaking the hillside.

"Get me out of here, Lacey. There must be a way!"

"There must be a—a key," she said.

Her voice trembled, making Tristan turn to look at her. Despite all her bluster, he knew Lacey was afraid of Gregory.

"Gregory must be watching too," Lacey continued, her voice steadier. "I'll look in his pocket. I can carry and turn a key."

"Lacey, what would happen to you if he—?"

Before Tristan could finish his question, she faded into a purple mist and was gone.

IVY GAZED UP AT TRISTAN, HER HEART BREAKING. SHE had to reach him.

The base of the monument was made of granite, rising in three tiers, its smooth surfaces made slick by rain, with no decorative carving to hold on to. The first tier, four feet above the ground, was too high for her to kneel on. Planting her hands on the shelf of stone, she jumped and used her locked arms to lift herself up. Her hands slipped on the wet surface. Sliding off, she scraped her arm along the stone edge from elbow to wrist and bit back a cry of pain.

"Ivy!"

"I'm here."

Drying her hands on the inside of her shirt, she tried again. This time she succeeded.

The next tier was shorter, and she could raise her knee high enough to get on it, but the ledge was even narrower than the one she was standing on.

"Ivy!"

She could hear Tristan's agony in the raggedness of his voice. "I'm here," she called back to him. "I'm coming."

She moved torturously slow. One tiny shift of weight in the wrong direction, one slip on the wet surface . . .

She was sitting on the second tier, with one foot tucked under her. The ledge was too narrow for both. She rose carefully to a staggered stance. The wind and rain whipped her clothes. She looked up at Tristan. He grimaced with pain.

"Oh, love, I'm almost there," she said.

"I'm going to die, Ivy."

"No. No, you're not!"

Seven feet up, seven to go. Ivy stood on her toes. Her fingers could almost touch the round base of the statue, but the narrow ledge made it impossible to get to the next tier. Yet somehow she had to!

The end of a coil of rope, part of the ropes that bound Tristan, was knotted at the base of the statue and hung loose below it, dancing in the wind tantalizingly close to her fingertips.

It was the only way: Jump, grab it, pull herself up. Flexing her knees, Ivy trained her eyes on it and leaped. Her hand reached wildly, grasping nothing but air. She banged her shoulder against the vertical rock, caught an edge with her foot, and tumbled to the ground.

For a moment she lay stunned, the breath knocked out of her. Above her, Tristan screamed in pain, and she struggled to her feet. Her foot kicked something, a small but heavy object. She leaned down, groping in the wet grass. Her fingers felt the barrel, then the handle of a gun.

"Ivy—Ivy, look—" Tristan called, his voice weak and broken up by the wind. "For the gun."

"I have it."

"Use it. . . . Kill me." His words came slowly, as if he was fighting for each breath.

"Tristan, I can't!"

"I'm begging you, Ivy. Finish it! *Please.*"

She stared at the gun in her hands.

"It's no sin, Ivy. It's kindness. If you love me, please!"

Tears streamed down Ivy's cheeks. She couldn't bear for him to be in such pain. "Tristan, you're fallen. If you die—"

"There's no greater hell than my life now," he cried. "Kill me! Then kill yourself, and we will be together forever."

Kill me. . . . Then kill yourself. Ivy silently repeated the words. She took a step back. "Tristan?" she asked softly, uncertainly.

"Here."

It sounded like his voice, but—

"Help me, Ivy!"

She took another step back, gazing up at the monument, then she turned and searched the gravestones around her. Her Tristan might ask to die—excruciating pain drove people toward death. But he would never ask her to kill herself, to give up her soul. This nightmarish vision was Gregory's. "Angel of love, free me," she prayed.

Lightning flashed. In the strobe-lit rain, she saw a pure white angel at the top of the monument, her arm raised and hand pointing toward heaven. No Tristan. No rope. Just an angel.

"Ivy!"

Tristan's voice came from another direction. Ivy dropped the gun and spun around. She saw a purple shimmer hovering at the door of a mausoleum. The padlock securing the door's latch fell to the ground. "Lacey!"

The shimmer moved away quickly as the door burst open. Ivy and Tristan ran to each other.

Tristan gathered her in his arms, sheltering her. "Oh my God! You're safe. I was watching you, calling you. I couldn't break through to you."

"I thought you were dying." Ivy cried. "I didn't know how to save you, Tristan."

"I love you, Ivy. I love you with my whole heart and soul. I will never let you go!"

She pressed her face against his chest. He was alive, his heart beating strongly. They had defeated Gregory at his own game. The storm was passing. They were going to make it through this.

Then Lacey shouted to them: "Get out of here. Now!"

Ivy turned and saw Lacey's purple mist hovering at the base of the monument. Gregory had emerged from beneath the dark tree and was running toward them.

"The gun!" Tristan raced toward the statue.

Gregory got there first and snatched up the weapon, pointing it at Tristan. "Don't move."

Ignoring Gregory's command, Ivy rushed forward.

"Get back, Ivy!" Tristan barked.

Gregory lowered the barrel of the gun. "No. No, let her come," he said, his voice turning soft, insinuating. His eyes burned with a peculiar gray-green light. "Come join us, Ivy. Isn't this nice? We're all together again. Just like old times."

Ivy took Tristan's hand.

Holding the gun at chest level, Gregory began to circle them. "I have to confess, I'm disappointed," he said. "I had planned it so well. It would have soothed my soul, Ivy, to watch you kill a dream, then despair and turn the gun on yourself. Your devoted Tristan here—after watching you die like that, he, too, would have killed himself. And the three of us could have been together eternally. What a shame!"

Gregory stopped circling and moved toward them, backing them toward his grave. The thunder was just a low rumble now. The rain had stopped, though the branches of the massive tree still drizzled on them.

Continually stepping backward, Tristan tried to keep Ivy behind him. Suddenly, he turned his head to the side.

"What is it?" she whispered.

"The voices," he answered just as softly.

"Telling secrets?" Gregory asked, sounding amused. "The voices know all the secrets that matter. Do you hear them, Tristan? The voices are murmuring her name, *Ivy, Ivy.*"

Goose bumps rose along Ivy's arms.

"Who are they talking to?" Gregory baited Tristan. "You or me? Listen: *The power is within you.*"

"You have no power," Ivy said. "You are your own parasite, Gregory. You are both hookworm and host, your self-love devouring your own soul."

Gregory straightened like a serpent raising its head, ready to strike. Fury darkened a web of veins in his neck. His eyes burned like gray embers.

Tristan pushed Ivy away from him. "Run!" he shouted. "Run!"

Charging Gregory, he knocked the gun from his hands. He and Gregory dove for it, then Tristan grabbed the weapon and took aim.

"No!" Ivy cried.

Tristan squeezed the trigger.

"Tristan, no!"

The gun did not discharge. For a moment all three stood still.

Ivy gasped with relief. "Lacey," she said, remembering the purple shimmer at the base of the monument—Lacey had removed the bullets.

Filled with rage, Gregory attacked Tristan. Pounding each other with fists, they tumbled onto Gregory's grave. Gregory kneeled on Tristan and held him by the neck. His hands were strong—the same hands that had beaten and strangled others. Tristan struggled for breath and pushed back, using his own powerful arms. He shifted the balance, rolling Gregory to the side, fighting to get on top.

"Run, Ivy!" he cried out.

But Ivy didn't move. If Tristan died a fallen angel, or if Tristan killed—*Angels, show me how to save him.*

A wind rose up, blowing away the remnants of the storm. Stars shone through tattered clouds.

Ivy remembered the starlit night she had risen to Tristan. She could still feel on her lips his life-giving kiss. Tristan, forgetting his angelic nature, had loved too much in a human way. He still did. He'd save her at the peril of his soul.

Angels, help us.

Suddenly, Ivy saw things she had never seen before. The sun waiting below the horizon. The police cars arriving at the cemetery gates. The tearing roots of the huge beech.

And Ivy knew: For Tristan to be redeemed, they had to return to what was meant to be the day that Tristan died, the breaking of their earthly bond. Somehow, Ivy had to find the courage to let go *for* him.

She heard a voice she hadn't heard since she was a small child. *God's love is within you.*

With those words came unworldly strength. Ivy rushed forward and pushed Tristan away from Gregory. The ground quaked, rising beneath Tristan, throwing him to his knees, forcing him beyond the shadow of the tree. Then Ivy rested a hand on Gregory and pointed upward.

The tree tilted. Gregory stared at it, his mouth gaping with terror as the massive trunk and limbs pitched toward him and Ivy.

Ivy called out, "I love you Tristan, now and everafter," then she saw through the tree to the brilliant stars.

TRISTAN CLAWED THE EARTH, TRYING TO CRAWL across the heaving ground, but couldn't reach Ivy. He heard her words. He watched with horror as the tree fell.

Everafter

Someone sobbed.

"Everafter. Everafter," he repeated, his heart refusing to make sense of what his eyes saw. The trunk of the beech had crushed Gregory. Ivy lay motionless, dead, her gold hair caught under a heavy limb. Bending over Ivy, Lacey cried as if her heart had broken in a million pieces.

Nineteen

THE TREES WERE BARE NOW, THE EXQUISITE ARCHI-
tecture of their branches etched against the town houses
and high-rises lining Washington Square. Beth leaned
against Will, the two of them sitting on a bench, Will
drawing the NYU students and busy New Yorkers cutting
through the park.

It had been the hardest three months of Beth's life.
If given the choice, she would have chosen to have
both Gregory and Ivy in her world, rather than lose her
friend. But the spirit of Gregory was gone—the body of

Bryan buried—and Ivy far beyond them now.

Tristan's father, Reverend Carruthers, had been a huge help to them. He knew something about coming through bewildering grief and opening himself up to unexpected possibilities, even happiness. He and Dr. Carruthers had opened their hearts and home, taking in the falsely accused "Luke McKenna"—the evidence Ivy had pursued had exonerated him. They believed they were giving him the kind of family life he had never known before.

Maggie and Andrew were selling the big house on the hill—too many memories. They lived in town now. Philip could easily ride his bicycle to Tristan's house, as well as to Beth's and Will's when they were home from college. Beth's heart had ached for Philip and Tristan, and none of them would have made it through the loss without Lacey. Lacey had witnessed Ivy's prayer; she had seen what Ivy saw, and had helped them make peace with Ivy's choice.

It had been much harder for Suzanne to find peace in the loss. She had come home to a very different world than the one she'd left. She argued passionately against Ivy's sacrifice. Little by little, Beth had been telling her the story of their summer, hoping that eventually Suzanne would understand how Ivy had followed her heart to the end and seen past Now to Everafter.

Kelsey, too, had been badly shaken by Ivy's death, as well as the revelation of Bryan's crimes. Like Max, Kelsey was in the nearly impossible situation of both grieving for and being horrified by a person who had become deeply entwined in her life. She had shocked her parents by giving up her ticket to a Florida university and attending a college close to home, a school she could commute to for the first semester.

Dhanya had also surprised her parents, but, Beth thought, she probably wouldn't have surprised Ivy with her new strength and independence. She continued with her plan to attend Wellesley, which was not so far from Boston College, where Max was going. She and Max had become close while trying to cope with Ivy's and Bryan's deaths. She now described herself and Max as "best friends." Beth smiled to herself: Surprising and wonderful things could happen when you were the best of friends with a guy.

And Chase—Beth smiled again—was Chase, back at school and searching for answers to all he'd been through, or rather, becoming "an expert" in Eastern mysticism.

"I love it when you smile like that," Will said to Beth, lifting his pencil from his sketchpad, bending his head to look at her. "I've got my own Mona Lisa!" He kissed her gently.

"Will, I've been wondering. . . . Lacey was with us day and night the week after Ivy died. But we haven't seen her since. Neither has Tristan or Philip—I texted Philip this morning and asked him. Do you think that *we* could have been Lacey's mission? Do you think she's moved on to the Light?"

Will considered it. "She sure acted like an angel that week." He started to sketch again, adding to his city scene a girl in a tank top, leggings, and booties. Then he closed the spiral pad.

"I miss Lacey," Beth said.

"Me too. A lot."

They got up to walk, Will's arm around Beth, her arm around him, and were nearly run over by someone weaving down the sidewalk on a unicycle. The girl spun around, winked at them, then took off again, looking like just another offbeat New Yorker, her purple hair whipping in the breeze.

"THIS IS MY FAVORITE PLACE ON CAPE COD," PHILIP said.

"Is it?" Tristan sat next to him on the landing halfway down the fifty-five steps to the beach. The heavy green that had covered the bluff was dry and woody now; the grasses on the dunes, thin. Tristan gazed out at the deep blue sky of early November, then his eyes followed the sweep of sea around the point and through the inlet to his and Ivy's harbor. "Why?"

"You're kind of in the sky," Philip explained. "It feels like angels could stop here to rest. Do you think Ivy and Lacey stop here much?"

The question caught Tristan by surprise. After Lacey had left, Philip had waited for Ivy to come back to him as an angel he could see and hear. Tristan had done everything he could to fill up those moments of disappointment, to ease Philip's pain. Tristan believed that Ivy had immediately gone on to the Light. He no longer heard the voices. Each day he found some way to move forward, redeeming himself, believing they would be together again when time became everafter.

"I don't know, Philip."

"Do you think Ivy's looking down on us, watching just in case we need help?"

"Maybe." He would not lie to Philip, but he would not discount a child's or anyone else's belief. No one had all the answers.

"I miss her."

"I love her," Tristan said.

They spoke at the same time; it eased Tristan's heart.

"And you know what?" Tristan added. "I love you, too."

"I know."

He smiled at Philip's unaffected certainty.

Philip started down the steps. "I think," he said, "that Ivy and Lacey are having a really good time together."

Tristan laughed out loud, imagining an angelic version of a buddy film, the kind with the two cops who never appeared to get along but actually had each other covered.

He followed Philip across the narrow boardwalk and through the dunes to the sea. Andrew and his father had been right: Coming back here with family helped with the healing.

Tristan and Philip walked for a long time at the edge of the ocean, Philip dancing about, dodging the foamy water, trying to pick up shells before the waves caught them. He stuffed his pockets with stones and shells, then when they reached the steps again, dumped them out. He wasn't the little kid Tristan had met more than two years ago; he still wanted to look at everything—touch everything—but he no longer had to take everything home with him.

Philip ran up the steps, taking them two at a time, as if to show Tristan that his legs were getting longer. At the landing he stopped to catch his breath, then bent over to look at something.

"I knew it! I knew it!" Philip straightened up, his face as bright as the sun. "Tristan, come here!"

Before Tristan had reached the final step, Philip stretched out his hand. In his palm lay a gold coin engraved with an angel, the one that Philip had placed in the hands of his sister the last time the three of them were together.

Tristan touched it. "Ivy," he said softly. Her name on his lips would always feel like an angelic kiss.

Acknowledgments

MANY OF THE SETTINGS IN THIS TRILOGY ARE REAL, such as the towns, parks, and beaches. Some—the inn, homes, churches, and secondary streets—are based on real places, but have been moved to new locations, built upon, and renamed, so that I could weave a good story. Still other places exist only in my mind: The real city of Providence is a wonderful place to live and to visit; the neighborhood of River Gardens sprang up from my imagination.

Thanks once again to Karen and Mac of The Village Inn, who provided excellent tips as I researched settings and who made me so comfortable at their Cape Cod B&B. Thanks to my sister, Liz, and her husband, Nick, who live on the Cape and have given me lots of great ideas. Liz, thank you, for all that driving, leaving me free to look.

I owe thanks to another family member, Gregory. Six books ago, when I needed a name for my villain, I borrowed that of my much-loved cousin so that I would write more positively about this character and not give away too quickly how evil he was. Let me just say that my cousin does not look anything like the villainous Gregory, nor does he act like him—though as a child he was a bit devilish. I thank him not only for his name, but for being a skilled sailor who responds to questions such as *where's a good place to dump a body,* and *how do I overturn a boat?* If there are any nautical errors in these books, they are mine, not his (writers can get so poetic!).

Thank you to my sister-in-law and niece, Sharyn and Abbie. Your enthusiasm keeps me going! Thanks to my parents, who have always been so supportive.

A huge thank-you goes to my superb editor. I wish I could find a more original way to say this, because it is no exaggeration: These three books would not have been possible without Emilia Rhodes. I am so grateful for her insights into characters and motivation, her talent for brainstorming, her ability to put her finger on the things that "bump" and to figure out why they bump, her understanding of a book's architecture, her skill in prioritizing, and her unfailingly upbeat outlook. Thank you to Jen Klonsky and Josh Bank for teaming us up and letting us have at it.

Finally, thank you, Bob. Love ya!